Splatterpunk's Not Dead!

Edited by
Jack Bantry

SPLATTERPUNK ZINE
www.splatterpunkzine.wordpress.com

This collection © 2016 Splatterpunk Zine
Introduction © 2016 Jeff Burk
Cover illustration © 2016 Dan Henk

Another Bunch of Flowers by The Road
© 2016 Nathan Robinson
High Fashion © 2016 Robert Essig
Beware the Beverage © 2016 Jeff Strand
Eggbeater © 2016 Saul Bailey
Please Subscribe © 2016 Adam Cesare
Abstinence © 2016 Shane McKenzie
The Androgyne © 2016 Brendan Vidito
Walter's Last Canvas © 2016 Paul Shrimpton

All rights reserved.

ISBN: 1537257331
ISBN-13: 978-1537257334

For the splatter punks

Contents

Punk Is Horror: An Introduction by Jeff Burk	1
Another Bunch of Flowers By The Road by Nathan Robinson	4
High Fashion by Robert Essig	17
Beware the Beverage by Jeff Strand	30
Eggbeater by Saul Bailey	39
Please Subscribe by Adam Cesare	53
Abstinence by Shane McKenzie	66
The Androgyne by Brendan Vidito	74
Walter's Last Canvas by Paul Shrimpton	82
Contributors	101

Acknowledgments

Thanks to everyone who has contributed to the anthology, bought a copy, reviewed it, or just given it a big up. I know who you all are!

- Jack Bantry

Punk is Horror: An Introduction

Jeff Burk

John Skipp, one of the founding members of the original splatterpunk movement, said in a YouTube interview, "people concentrate on the 'splatter' but forget the 'punk.'"

It seems that many associate the horror genre with metal music. I can understand why on a surface level. The subject matter of monsters and gore is often similar between the two genres. But while metal presents a rebellious image, the genre is really about careful craftsmanship. When one looks over the history of the horror genre, it isn't technical perfection that is most remembered, but unrestrained passion.

Personally, I've always believed that horror was more similar to punk rock. Punk encourages its audience to get out into the world and create their own art. That's just where many of the best voices in horror have come from. Even though I pursued a path of literature, it was horror legends like Sam Raimi, Peter Jackson, and Troma Studios that inspired me to just do it myself.

It was also the punk scene that gave us zines - small, hand-stapled and photocopied booklets that proved a forum for niche voices that would otherwise never be published. And the horror scene once again took notice. Through the eighties and nineties, handmade zines were a way that many small press authors managed to get an audience. Writers such as Brian Keene, Edward Lee, and Carlton Mellick III all started as hopefuls with Xeroxed zines and are now major voices in the genre.

Once the internet revolution really took hold and web "publications" became a serious option, the handmade zines just seemed to disappear. It makes sense - while zines did have a relatively low cost, websites were even lower. There was no need for postage, anyone in the world with internet access could see whatever you had to show.

But there was something missing. Those old zines were a labor of love. There was a personal touch, from the way that each paragraph had to be carefully designed to how the very structure of the pages being assembled was done by hand. You knew holding the zine, that whoever made it did it with passion.

Thank god for Jack Bantry remembering that and giving us the Splatterpunk Zine. For four years and seven issues, Bantry has given the fans of hardcore horror a publication that radiated love and joy for the genre. And the genre was waiting for someone like him to come along. We were all ready for it, whether we knew it or not. Over the course of just a few issues, Bantry has been able to give us a publication that repeatedly delivered on representing the biggest names in horror fiction and the most promising newcomers.

Now at this point you're probably like, "that's all well and fucking good but this ain't no hand stapled zine, this is a fucking book!"

I congratulate you on being so observant.

The Dead Kennedys, Minor Threat, and Crass started off just as wild nobodies and released seven-inches through basically pocket change but they grew into Alternative Tentacles Records, Dischord Records, and Crass Records. Sometimes it turns out you're really fucking good at your passion.

That's where we now find ourselves with Splatterpunk. What started as just a small zine, has built itself a loyal fan base and is consistently a must read publication for fans of fucked-up horror.

Frequently, a step up in professionalism goes hand-in-hand with a loss of edge. I don't worry about that here. I don't believe Bantry is going to forget the "splatter" or the "punk."

Another Bunch of Flowers by the Road

Nathan Robinson

It had to be a Monday. Monday morning rush hour, it would fuck up the rest of the week that way.

The carnage, the terror and everything else. This was his requiem, and they'd all join in his song whether they liked it or not.

He flicked the switch, and with a lightning stuttering of fluorescents, the machine was revealed to his eyes. He'd completed it last Thursday, but gave himself the weekend off to enjoy a few final things; a steak, a movie, a walk on the beach, simple things that used to delight him. He even sat on a bench outside a school on Friday afternoon, taking in what joy he could from the squealing laughter of the children as they enjoyed their last play.

It had to be a Monday, so he wasn't losing anything in spending a bit of time away from the project.

But he'd done it with time to spare.

In the realm of possibilities, he never thought this would come to be, thinking he would've been hampered by time or money or just plain old giving up.

No.

He'd seen it through.

He'd even sprayed it entirely black to complete its look of mechanical oblivion.

It had come to him in a dream of fire and death and destruction. He awoke with the taste of petrol stinging his lips, and he hurriedly found a scrap of paper and sketched out a design, trying his best to remember the details of his dream.

He'd seen where the bodies went in.

Now it was a premonition made real. The metal beast stood before him, a gleaming testament to his efforts. Deep down he knew that this wasn't some psychotic delusion born from grief, but a genuine need for revenge against society itself and everything it stood for. He wasn't a terrorist by any stretch and he'd been quite normal and boring up until this point. He'd never been in a fight, never sought to harm anyone else and during his twenties, even toyed with the idea of becoming a vegan. This wasn't a slight against anyone in particular but a strike out against humanity in general. This wasn't for religious reasons, in order to appease some sneering deity. He was there to prove a point, nothing more. He didn't care who died. He'd lost enough already. He was owed this. He couldn't see any way around this grief. This was his only gateway out. A final fuck you to the cruel world. A middle finger turned back before he blazed on into the sunset.

Life had been good, he'd been so damned happy. But then, a life shattered and plunged into a deep well of grief. He'd given up on the concept of having a name or identity, abandoning the notion when his family had been presented to him as shredded and carbonised corpses, becoming another bunch of flowers by the road. The only time he saw his name and it struck some sort of resonance was on letters and delivery notes. He wasn't a person anymore, merely a vessel of sadness carrying on memories of a family gone to dust and smoke and painful memories.

The insurance payout did nothing to counteract the despair, no matter how many zeros they stuck on the end. He felt like giving it all away and killing himself as he had nothing left to give. Starting another family was incomprehensible, as the terror was evident that it could happen all over again. Lightning does strike twice. Sometimes it strikes the same place on the same day, as he'd learnt. How could he marry again, knowing that everything beautiful either fades to dust or is smashed without warning? How could he even contemplate having children ever again when he'd experienced (thrice-fold) the unbearable and shattering event of losing everything he held dear?

This was more than revenge. This was proof that life is unfair and unjust and that we all live in a godless universe where the only guarantee was death (it was now fashionable for some folk to avoid tax, so that was struck off as one of life's certainties.) He was perpetuating in pain, passing it for others to taste, as if doing so would dilute his own.

He moved over to the roller door and unclipped the chain, pulling it down with a generous tug, the shutter furling up, revealing his creation to the brilliant blue skies beyond. It was a beautiful day so far.

He'd sold his home not long after the dream and sought out the rented workshop afterwards. He cut off ties with what distant family he had left and moved into one of the offices, spending his mostly sleepless nights curled up on a single mattress.

With the insurance pay out and the money from the house sale (the mortgage was only a few years from being completely paid off, they'd come close to winning the rat race), he could live quite comfortably without having to work. He had cash and he had time. He put both to good use.

Climbing up into the cab, he shivered. Anticipation? Fear? No, something new, more than excitement. Joy of a dream realised perhaps? This was it. For the first time in a long time, he was genuinely happy.

He stocked up with everything he needed the previous week. Water, petrol, propane, improvised explosives.

Before the accident, he'd been an engineer, so his particular set of skills had come in useful in realising his dream. He knew how to weld and suppliers of whatever equipment he needed could be found quite easily on the internet. His dream hadn't been too much trouble.

Inside the cab, he removed a picture of his wife and children from the pocket of his overalls, placing it in a joining gap on the control panel. Drenched in eternal sunlight, they smiled back at him.

From forever.

He pulled the door shut, bolting it tight and padlocking it to prevent it from opening. He hadn't included a handle on the outside. It wasn't designed to be opened from out there. He didn't want anyone getting in. That was the point. He didn't need a weapon to protect himself. He was the weapon.

I am the weapon. I offer no quarter today.

He sighed, and then drew a deep breath in order to compose his trembling.

You've come too far to go back. This is it.

He flicked a switch and four flat screens flickered to life. He pressed START ENGINE, and the beast snarled, then grumbled to life.

Starting with a chassis from a JCB and working up from that, he reinforced the underneath and welded sheets of steel to the sides, essentially turning the cab into a metal tomb, an amateur exoskeleton designed to carry the depressed lump of meat that he'd become. He installed CCTV forward, side and behind, giving him a view of what was outside without the use of windows. He even went to the extreme of installing his own ventilation system with backup oxygen tanks. Just in case.

It was time, he was ready. Taking the wheel, he dipped

the clutch and slipped it into gear, pulling forward out of the workshop, for the first and final time. This was the test. He wasn't turning back. He once read that humans should take two things from war. One was to forgive; the other was to learn where they went wrong.

None of these applied to him.

There didn't seem any need to close the door behind him.

He'd picked that specific workshop for its proximity to the off ramp for his soon to be favourite road. It was less than a two minute drive. Cars stopped and screeched as he headed towards the exit, drivers shaking fists and offering up particular fingers in response to seeing the strange machine barrel past them on this otherwise calm, blue-skied Monday morning.

He ignored them, and turned the exit into an entrance, descending down into the oncoming traffic.

He pulled a lever and the modified bucket lowered to within a few inches of the tarmac. He'd constructed a framework around the bucket, and then bolted thin sheets of steel on top to create a thirty-degree slope that slightly leant off to the left. He thumbed a button, and the "Road Saw," a five-foot wide blade began to whir. Cannibalised from another machine designed for slicing large swathes of concrete, he inverted the mechanism and built it in so it sat emerging centrally from a gap in the slope like a single, revolving snaggle tooth.

This was the primary weapon. But he had others.

A Fiat Punto leaving the main road and heading up the off ramp saw his approach and swerved onto the hard shoulder.

He altered his course, and sensing imminent danger, the driver of the Fiat sped up to try to get past him. They made it so far but risked crashing into the barrier.

The front tyre of the Fiat caught the front slope and immediately accelerated then flipped off the edge and then over the metal barrier, wheels revving as it tumbled down the slope.

Inside the cab, he laughed as a burst of adrenalin surged through him. There'd be others.

A second vehicle travelled up the slope, immediately braking at the sight of the flipped Fiat. It was a Mercedes Sprinter van. It turned hard, then started reversing to turn back the way they'd come.

He pushed on and charged the van before it had managed a one eighty. The driver threw his hands up as the bottom of the slope hit the wheel and tipped the laden van towards the saw.

He heard a crunch of metal, the shatter of glass and a human scream parted over the shriek of the blade turning through screaming metal and silent bone. He pushed on, weaving to and fro to dislodge the van as momentum carried it up the slope and off the side, the driver's door parted from the hinges, blood dripping from the torn interior. More vehicles greeted him, brakes smoking and screaming as bumpers kissed and split plastic in a tumble trip of bangs and shrieking bends.

Some had already tried to turn, but it was too late. He was on them. He didn't even get the make of the first car as it travelled directly up the slope and onto the spinning blade. Sparks flew as the blade ate through the front grill, into the bottom of the engine with a terrifying roar. The vehicle shook as the blade carried on through the passenger side, the next car pushing it off the slope as it met a similar fate. Petrol splashed up with blood as he tore the car in two.

He did the same for the next three, the hungry blade mindlessly devouring into the smorgasbord of protesting metal and reluctant flesh in a flurry of sparks and screams. His grin widened as he felt a rush of glee. This was fun. This was how it was supposed to be, blood as therapy.

Joining the main carriageway, cars immediately began swerving, most headed for the safety of the shoulder and the verge beyond. Others stopped dead, tyres shrieking in staggered unison as they pulled up diagonal to the white lines. Bumpers met bumpers, as the cars formed a coloured concertina of mayhem.

Sticking to the central lane, he ploughed the machine into them with vehement joy, delighting at each twist of metal. Every crunch was music, every scream joining the choir of avenging angels. To some it would seem this was madness, to him, it was healing.

He carried on; a hundred metres, a mile, another, leaving a trail of upturned devastation in his wake. Fires had started sending snakes of black smoke pleading into the sky, lost limbs twitched free of their bodies like electrified doll parts. A pair of legs, complete with Nikes and odd socks kicked out from the knees at the concrete central reservation.

This was all behind him now.

Fire.

Blood.

His family.

Ahead, blue flashing lights formed a dazzling line beneath the next bridge. He doubted they were here to talk him down or offer him sympathy. He was beyond that. Grief had taken him too far.

He'd expected this and decreased his speed even though he was clear of traffic from the roadblock ahead. He needed a moment to consider.

On the other side, traffic still flowed. Some zoomed, others rubbernecked. He stopped, letting the diesel engine idly grumble like a dragon catching its breath.

Placing his hand on a different set of controls, he began working a so far unused part of machinery.

From behind the cab, an arm drew up, flexing out with the grace of a mantis leg. The massive pneumatic breaker on the end reached out and pressed against the concrete barrier. With a thumbed switch, it began to pulse and punch, chewing into the low wall with spits of dust and shrapnel. Within thirty seconds, the concrete had split, the barrier pushed back. The blue lights ahead began to rush towards him, but it was too late, the barrier had been breached. Steering the arm forward, he punched the two pieces through to the other side then reversed through the gap.

Horns blared and tyres squealed as the metal beast emerged into the fast lane with all the grace of a blind dinosaur. With a twist of the wheel, he turned the contraption into traffic and began a fresh chapter of chaos as a prospective rubbernecker sent his Mondeo up the ramp, into the saw and exploding over the top in a fury of sparks and spitting fuel. In the next moment, the spray of fuel caught an ember of burning metal, a fiery cushion blooming as the car crash landed. A Subaru jumped the ramp, missing the saw and pirouetting over the side, landing on its roof and skidding toward the awaiting flames. A Land Rover was next, the bull bars caught on the blade and flipped over itself, sending it cartwheeling over the top in a flip of jarring death that would snap spines and necks.

The carnage continued, metal kissing metal in grinding smacks, glass bursting and exploding into plagues of false diamonds. The screams fought to be noticed over the trail of hissing fuels tanks igniting and making funeral pyre bonfires of the eviscerated car wrecks. Blooming mushroom clouds followed, as if he fertilised the ground, giving rise to their devastating fruition.

Inside the cab, he was laughing, his guffaws echoing bluntly off his metal surroundings. With each vehicle bouncing up the ramp, he felt a rush of cool blood run through him, chilling and exciting him. The following crashes he left behind added further to the delightful chaos.

This was his show, his delightful revenge, and not an ounce of guilt weighed against his crushed soul. Car crash catharsis.

The cars ahead began to slow, pulling over on to the

hard shoulder in an effort to clear out of his path, bunching up and locking bumpers. One plucky motorist managed a U-turn and headed the wrong way down the hard shoulder before crashing headlong into a coach, embedding in four seats deep.

He ploughed into the bunched traffic with glee, cars folding over the edge of the ramp and flipping onto their roofs. Every third vehicle or so, he'd hit dead on, aiming for the fuel tank, spilling explosive juices. The sparks took care of the rest as he left the flames behind.

Ahead, dark figures were crouched above on a bridge. He caught them on his screen and assumed them to be onlookers.

A loud ping against the metal body told him otherwise.

A second ping and the screen to his front camera went black.

He tapped the screen in effort to revive it, but it remained dead.

A third and fourth ping quickly resonated.

The police had brought guns, and now he was forward blind. He accelerated, pushing through the jungle of stalled cars. On the other screens he could see bodies fleeing their vehicles in a mad dash for the safety beyond the barrier, scrambling over and falling with relief into the detritus and brambles. They can go, he thought, with the knowing will of a kind god.

He approached the bridge, slowing before he reached it. He thumbed more switches, checked the connections and then turned an unmarked dial implemented for his own design.

A breath of flame burst up from a skyward facing nozzle on the roof, licking the railing with all the ferocity of a dragon's tongue. He couldn't see the results of his actions, but he heard the screams.

Strangely, and for first time in a long while, he found himself hard. Not by way of arousal, but because of the coursing life in his veins finding its way into every thin corner of his being. He gripped it, half proud, half ashamed. It shouldn't be. But it was.

He let go of himself and opened a small front hatch, enabling him to see the way ahead, and pressed the accelerator.

The road was clear enough for vehicles to manage U-turns without catastrophic incident. The traffic had all but vanished in the next mile, aside from a Volvo, with all four doors open, the interior devoid of life apart from a caged Alsatian spinning circles in a cage in the rear of the car.

Being a compassionate man, he let the dog be and trundled onwards.

Again, blue lights blazed ahead. He narrowed his gaze as a police car screamed down towards him. It stuck close to the hard shoulder as it approached, so he edged closer to intervene. In the last thirty feet, it diverted, pulling hard in the opposite direction and missing the ramp by less than a foot. He heard the tyres squeal as it braked hard behind him. He watched on the screen as it jolted to a stop.

Without hesitation he grasped hold of the breaker control and reached the arm out toward the police car as he backed up towards it. The breaker pushed through the top edge of the bonnet and under the dash. The windscreen imploded. He raised the arm high and then swung over to the other side, stopping the rotation with a jolt. The car slipped off the end of the breaker and landed on the central barrier, bending and forming around the concrete.

On the screen, a blurry body fell out from the passenger side, stumbling over the barrier and towards him. He jabbed down with the breaker, indenting the tarmac. The black-clad figure dodged the arm, rolled and ended up behind him. He watched as the hero climbed up to the main body.

'It's over fella, they're blocking off the exits, come on out, okay? No more, yeah? Give it up.' The cop was inches away.

Inside, he turned a different nozzle. Flames jetted out from the base of the cab, creating a ring of fire. He heard the hero scream, cursing over the rising hiss. He pushed the accelerator, watching the rear video for the hero to fall onto the road.

He remained unseen.

He turned the valve again, letting the fire breathe out in hot, twisting plumes that trailed behind like broken fingers.

He turned the wheel to and fro in an effort to dislodge his stowaway, to no avail. He straightened up and turned the valve off, braking sharp and throwing it into reverse. He braked again.

Still the cop remained hidden.

He pushed forward again. Aside from getting out and confronting his passenger, there wasn't much he could do.

He pushed on. Towards to the line of blue lights. Determined to break through them and carry on his crusade.

He had a point to prove and he intended to make it known that he was pissed off. Life hadn't been kind, so why should he show any kindness in return? After all he'd been through; wreaking revenge against strangers was the only compensation he could see as true justice, as if causing pain somehow detracted from suffering his own despair and anguish. He was blind to everything else.

So far, it seemed that the therapy was working. He felt no guilt, no fear and zero regret at what he had done. He felt lighter, brighter, relieved even.

They were meat, nothing more. Just things he was using to feel better. It wasn't like he'd have to suffer guilt. If he had to answer to a god on the other side, he'd give him what for.

On the rear camera, a dark figure flashed by, scuttling away and to the side of the road. He didn't chase the shambling figure.

Aside from his breath, silence filled the cab. His ears adjusted to the wave of sirens increasing. He looked out the front hatch, locking it a second later as the cars rushed towards him in a tsunami of twirling blue. They stopped, and bodies started to mill about.

It was over. They had him. He could go back, but what was the point? This had to end at some point. He'd imagined an ending like this; traditional Hollywood with the supposed bad guy facing down against the police. Even though HE KNEW that he was the good guy and the victim, society, the law and the media wouldn't see it like that. They'd understand he was a broken man, twisted by the loss of his family until he sought revenge against random strangers. That's exactly what it was, but until they'd experienced what he felt, the agony of loss, there wasn't any way that they'd understand. They'd remember him, he was sure of that.

He reached down into his bag and screwed the top off the bottle of Merlot. It was a cheap brand, but he and his wife had enjoyed it as a personal favourite during their marriage. He hadn't brought a glass, he didn't feel a need for decorum during his last minutes. He hadn't any witnesses to this. He was here to enjoy himself. He didn't care if he dribbled.

He looked at the photo on the console in front of him, smiling at his sun bathed family. He remembered that day, it had been a good one. The best.

He revved the engine and started up a gear, towards the line of defence that was in place to stop him.

Good Luck. I hope you win, because I'm on the last rung and my fingers are slipping. I wasn't meant to win. That's why I'm here. That's why you're here, to stop me losing anymore, and the only way I could possibly win would probably destroy the universe it's so damned unnatural. I can't take any more so I need you to take this away from me before I do anymore damage. You need to take the controls away because I'll carry on until I'm grinding metal. Now I think I've done enough and I could go on, but I'm tired. I've proved my point and I'm sick of it all. I've had my fun.

He opened the hatch. Ahead, he saw expectant tense

faces peer from behind police cars. They'd assembled a steep ramp, meant to halt his progress. It didn't matter. He leant down and twisted the nozzle of the gas canister, unclipping the hose so it filled the cab. Beneath the seat he'd cannibalised several boxes of fireworks, emptying their contents into cardboard boxes filled with nails and screws. It was crude, but he hoped it would do the trick. The three petrol canisters should help it along as well.

Lifting the bottle, he took a hearty glug, crimson dribbling down from the corner of his wet smile as a perverse delirium took over. He was crying as he picked up the picture of his family, wondering if he'd made the wrong choice, but knowing full well that it was too late. How could he come back from this? How could anyone?

He was sliding, yet his foot was pushed down on the accelerator with a self-destructive vehemence.

The stern faces behind the roadblock got closer and the rapid *ting ting* of bullets on the armour played sweet music to his ears.

He dropped the bottle of merlot and kissed the picture as he hit the faux incline. The gas brought nausea and churned the wine in his food free stomach making him feel sicker than he already was.

It was over. Here it comes.

He'd haunt this road, he was sure of it.

They'd remember him.

He'd be more than just another bunch of flowers by the road.

High Fashion

Robert Essig

Jordan rubbed his eyes like he was trying to push them into his skull.

Tension headache.

No, stress headache.

Samantha Waite—fashion guru, founder of Waite Fashion—rolled her eyes. "Look, Jordy, I know you don't like hearing this, but I don't mince words. Your designs are promising, but they're just not up to snuff. Fashion is as changing as an ocean tide. You have to keep up with it or it'll wash you away. I really don't want to see you lose, Jordy. You have potential, but...."

"I know, I know, there's always a big but." Jordan sighed, irritated with the lashing she was handing him.

Samantha cringed. "You need to clean yourself up. You reek like a distillery, you know that?"

"Long night."

"It's always something, isn't it?"

"Look, Sam, you know my designs are good. I've won awards. My outfits have graced the catwalk *and* the red carpet."

"Yeah, that was two years ago. Waite Fashion did good by you back then. Made me proud to be your mentor, but lately you're on a downward spiral. I'm beginning to wonder if you still have it. These designs—" she grabbed a small stack of papers with dresses sketched in colored pencil. "They're uninspired shit."

Jordan took a deep breath.

"Don't you sigh again," Samantha said. "You sound like a fucking hydraulic press."

He rolled his eyes instead.

"Look," Samantha said, "I'm giving you a month."

"What?"

"You work better under pressure. Maybe you should think about how you came up with those explosive designs that graced my line two years ago. I understand that artistic creativity can strike at different times for different reasons, but you have to know how to harness it. If you want to be a success in this business, then you had better learn how to produce."

Another young woman, whose father was the head of some film company or another, came up and asked Samantha a question. The girl was maybe twenty years old and because of her father's connections she would likely become something by default. Made Jordan sick.

Samantha was finished with him, at least for now. He liked her no nonsense approach to life in general, but being on the receiving end of her wrath was a drag. She was well respected. That she had taken him in when he was a stupid teenager with a dream had been a blessing, and perhaps he'd taken it too far. Maybe he had been leeching off of her all this time, thinking he was something when he was actually nothing.

Jordan slinked out of the building with the sick feeling that all eyes were on him and that everybody knew he'd been given an ultimatum. He stepped outside and wondered which bars were open at eight in the morning.

He was in no mood for going home and sulking over his sketchbooks. He liked a human canvas, not a mannequin, and he certainly did not like to sketch as so many other designers do.

After hailing a taxi, Jordan headed across town where he could maybe score some coke or even meth if it came to that. He'd found drugs to be the solution to just about everything, and when he thought about where his life had been a few years ago when he dreamed up those, how did Samantha say it, "explosive" designs, he knew one thing: he'd been knee deep in nose candy and clubbing like an eighteen year old American in Tijuana.

After dropping in on a reliable dealer who hooked him up with a dope bag for a blowjob, Jordan pulled a couple rails into his nostrils and headed back to his place where he spent the rest of the day trying to make the coke last into the night. He came up with another series of uninspired sketches, even used a mannequin, but felt more like stabbing his eyes with pins than using them to pin back material.

Night fell just as he finished his dope. Had he any money he would have bought more. He was sweaty, his eyes burned, and he experienced hot flashes followed by cool sensations. The apartment was getting stuffy.

After a shower and shave, Jordan headed to a club he used to frequent. Hadn't been there since he'd been trying to clean his act up, and that had subsequently led to a great bout of depression. He would rather sit at home with a gallon of vodka and some cranberry juice than show his face in public. He had this crazy notion that people would recognize him as the has-been who had a wonderful clothing line once upon a time.

Samantha's words had haunted him all day. He tended to ignore her when she chewed him out about his lifestyle or his drinking, but there was one thing she said that stuck with him. She'd mentioned something about him going back to where he'd been when he came up with his greatest designs. He'd racked his mind and found that the months had all blended together in an intoxicating soup of pharmaceuticals, booze, and loose men. Back then he was a man about town, cavorting around the clubs and taking names. He was confident, self-assured, and he believed in what he was doing. Nowadays he tried to believe, tried to convince himself that he had what it took to be a fashion mogul, but truth is he felt he lost whatever it was that he'd had. It must have been luck.

Samantha once told him that luck was a fallacy. She said you either have it or you don't and Jordan believed that.

The coke gave him confidence. Once he finagled his way into the club, he managed to talk his way into a few pills and some drinks. He knew all the regulars, and most of them liked him, were glad to see him after his lengthy absence.

Especially Kyle Knotts.

At first glance, Jordan wanted nothing to do with Kyle. They'd had a fling some time ago. About as serious a relationship as Jordan had ever been in. It ended badly and he was still bitter, but pills coursed through his veins and some guy offered him some special K and damn that stuff was special all right. Went right to Jordan's brain. He saw trails like oil slicks dancing before him. People exuded bright auras like glimmering fairies. This place—in his mind, not physically—was one he'd not been to in quite some time, and it felt good. It felt damn good.

For an instant, like an old-fashioned bulb-flash camera, he was stunned into sobriety. Kyle had a smile on his face like he was the most important guy in the room, like he had been asked to be there for the sake of his fans, if ever he had fans. More importantly, he looked absolutely fabulous. Not the clothes, not even the kooky hairdo, but his body.

A thumping dance beat replaced the temporary brilliance of heavenly trumpets that cascaded over Jordan's mind. Poison coursed through his veins and for a moment he felt like a zombie. It was as if his depression and self-loathing had culminated with the drugs into some kind of negative aura.

Kyle looked up and their eyes met. Kyle's smile didn't falter, and though Jordan would have liked to say the same, he knew the look on his face was either that of the stoned idiot who didn't know how to ride the high, or the depressed fool he felt deep within.

Or maybe not.

Kyle waded through the crowd of sweaty, eager dancing bodies, eyes looking up at Jordan's as if claiming his prize, making sure it didn't get away. Jordan didn't move. He just stared at this man he once loved. Was it true love? Was it from deep within? He wasn't sure, but Kyle always had an air of self-assuredness to him. Something, even when his spring line was hot, Jordan found difficult to achieve.

"Haven't seen you here in a while," Kyle said.

Jordan felt silly, like a schoolboy faced with his first crush. His mouth was dry (probably from the dope), and his senses dulled to the point of your average inbred hillbilly.

"I've been working," Jordan said.

"Oh, really. Your latest line?"

Did Jordan detect a morsel of condescension?

What came out of his mouth next was something that must have been fueled by everything he'd been going through matched with all of the mind-altering substances he'd been gorging himself on. In Kyle's aura he saw a mirror, and he talked as if he were making up conversation, saying the things he wanted to say without abandon.

"I *am* working on my new line, as a matter of fact." He smiled big and bright. Like a reflection. "Samantha Waite wants some designs for her fall collection. Thing is, I've been trying to dip into the pool of inspiration I had been wading in when I came up with those astonishing trends a few years back. You remember, right?"

Kyle, body grooving to the beat, nodded. "Yeah, I remember. But I haven't seen your name on anything since."

Jordan rolled his tongue across his lips like Cher and said, "Well you ain't seen nothin' yet. Thing is, I need that inspiration again. You know what that inspiration is?"

"Crystal meth, a bathtub of Jell-o, and two tranny hookers?"

Jordan laughed like he'd heard the best joke in the world and then cut to the chase in all the seriousness of a doctor reporting the untimely death of a loved one. "Funny, but no, the inspiration I'm talking about is you."

This took Kyle aback. For the first time in this conversation, the first they'd shared since breaking up almost two years ago, Kyle looked like he was lost for words.

"Come to my place?" Jordan asked.

Kyle had the body of a model. He was tall and lanky, so thin you assumed that whenever he went to the bathroom he was purging his last meal. He'd come to Jordan's apartment with the obvious desire for sex, considering the bulge showing in his underwear, however Jordan's lust at this moment was for fashion.

"Come on, Jordy, I don't want to wear that."

An overwhelming feeling of rejection smacked Jordan in the face. He stood there holding the very bra Kyle had cavorted around in back when they were an item—black with white polka dots—the one that gave him the appearance of a small bust, which was the precise touch needed to fill out Jordan's frantic designs, the ones that appeared in Samantha's fall line and earned him an article in *Cosmo*.

"Jeez, don't take it so hard," Kyle said. "I'm just not into that anymore. I guess you didn't hear, but I decided not to take the estrogen and I obviously haven't gone through with the operation."

"But..." Jordan was lost for words. His mind was whipping around like a candy wrapper caught in a dust storm. He shook, trembled, fought to keep his emotions in check. "Just once. Just for tonight. You know my motto: Live fast, die young, leave an exquisite corpse."

Kyle was no longer aroused. He looked frightened. "Okay. But first, make me a drink."

A smile threatened to peek from Samantha's normally stern, overworked face. "Jordy, Jordy, what have we here?"

Jordan was pleased to present a design for which he was tremendously proud. He'd used the fabric like a madman, cutting and altering, pinning and adjusting to Kyle's disdain. Kyle certainly had changed. Didn't enjoy the attention and praise of being a human model like he used to. But the design Jordan created on his body—with only two accidental pokes with a pin—was awe-inspiring.

The dress was now pinned back on a mannequin. He arrived to the warehouse early to prepare it before Samantha got there. That and he was speeding like a freight train and needed something to occupy his time. He'd made a sketch of the design before Kyle, in a fit if irritation, ripped off the cuts of fabric that had been pinned back over his body, showcasing Jordan's raw creativity. No matter how many sketches he'd done, trying to free the designs that were trapped in his mind, he had to have the human canvas of Kyle to work with to break the chains that bound his creativity. It had worked before, and by the response Samantha gave him, it appeared to have worked again.

She stood to the left and then to the right, looked the

fabric up and down, holding her chin in a way that indicated serious consideration. Had she not liked it, she would have rolled her eyes and ordered the fabric recycled. Probably would have told Jordan never to grace her mannequins with such atrocious rags.

"I like it," she said. It wasn't quite the response Jordan expected. "I want more like this." She looked Jordan in the eyes. Her face contorted like someone put a rotten fish under her nose. "You look like hell, Jordy. Up all night on this?"

"Yeah, pretty much."

"Get some sleep." She looked at the mannequin again. "I like this. It has flair, elegance, it's chic. I want more. I don't know what you did and I don't care. Sometimes you find your creative foothold and realize that there's only one way to unlock the brilliance within your mind. If you've found it again, Jordy, don't let go."

Kyle was hardly in any shape to drive or even walk, so Jordan did his best to act as a crutch for his old friend as they hobbled down the street from the club.

"Must've drank too much," Kyle slurred.

"Almost home," said Jordan.

By the time they made it into Jordan's apartment, Kyle collapsed onto the floor then crawled to a couch where he did his best to sit up, unable to do so. He kept flopping over like his spine was made of jelly.

"I think," Kyle said between his eyes closing as if from extreme fatigue, "Someone ... put something ... in my ... drink."

Jordan prepared fabrics and located his sheers. From his position on the floor, like a mad genius amongst the tools of his trade, he looked up at Kyle passed out on the couch. He'd never had a reason to use GHB before, but wow did it make a person vulnerable.

Jordan tried unsuccessfully to get Kyle to stand. He tickled him, told him a dirty joke, even grabbed his package hoping to arouse him and maybe bring some cognizance into those listless eyes.

How the hell was he going to work with a mannequin that was about as lively as a fresh cadaver?

Standing back, Jordan grabbed the bottle of vodka he'd been working on. He was numb. Worked better in that state of mind. The alcohol seemed to balance the drug cocktail he'd been fueling himself with. In times such as this one, he had to stand back and have a drink, feel the burn, blink away the lack of sleep.

Problem was Kyle really did look dead.

Jordan's heartbeat accelerated. His mouth went dry. He just about dropped the bottle, but managed to place it upon a bookshelf without averting his glassy stare into Kyle's eerily open eyes. A fly landed on one of those unblinking eyes. The dead don't blink flies away.

An overwhelming instant of panic washed over Jordan. He rushed to Kyle and placed his ear to Kyle's chest. Jordan felt body heat, but that didn't mean Kyle was alive. If he had just died from an overdose he would still be warm.

A thumping heartbeat rattled through Jordan's ear. Good, Kyle was alive. Very alive. In fact...

Jordan pulled his head away. Sweat oozed out of his pores creating a shellac on his face. It wasn't Kyle's heartbeat he was hearing—it was his own and it was frantic.

Grabbing Kyle's ankles, Jordan pulled his body off of the couch, horrified at how loose his joints were, how his head lolled off the cushion and hit the throw rug like a fallen bowling ball.

This time Jordan pushed a couple of fingers into Kyle's neck, searching for his carotid artery. He felt nauseous, his mind spinning almost as if he'd consumed a preposterous amount of booze on an empty stomach. He couldn't be sure he felt a damn thing in Kyle's neck.

Jordan slapped Kyle's face. "Wake up, damn you! Wake up!"

Jordan shrank backwards, crawling into a sort of fetal position at the edge of the couch. Couldn't take his eyes off of Kyle, lying on the floor like someone waiting for a chalk outline.

After maybe two minutes Kyle made a noise and shifted. Jordan let out a breath that he seemed to have been holding the entire time. He stood and now it was quite clear that Kyle was indeed alive. His breathing was so shallow that it was difficult to detect.

"Oh...my...god," said Jordan. "You scared the shit out of me."

Kyle didn't respond. Just lay there, eyes now closed.

Feeling as if the high he'd spent most of his adult life chasing had completely vanished, Jordan chopped up a few lines on a side table next to the couch. He inhaled, rubbed his nose, made facial expressions like he was on the verge of overdose, then looked at Kyle lying there incapacitated. He was better this way. Wouldn't be able to bitch and complain. He'd done a lot of that last time. Almost became too distracting for Jordan to work.

Yes, Jordan thought, this will work out just fine.

Jordan stripped Kyle down to his skivvies and burned the midnight oil, working feverishly on his latest design.

"Good god, Jordy," Samantha said, "You look like you've been run over by a garbage truck, but this design is something to behold."

Jordan, sporting a five o'clock shadow and eyes that looked like they'd been dipped in blood, smiled halfheartedly.

The design was sketched on a piece of paper with colored pencils. The paper was smudged and torn as if it had taken two trains, a few buses and a taxi to get there.

"I want you to see something," said Samantha. "Follow me."

Jordan followed. She continued to speak as they walked into her studio.

"I took your last design and personally sewed a prototype." She pulled a sheet off of a mannequin to reveal the dress. "I think there are a few things we can tweak, but I can see this one on the runway."

"It's beautiful," said Jordan, circling the dress, imagining his name on the tag.

"You're doing good work, Jordy. Keep it up. I like seeing you working again. This world needs Jordy Theaker."

With every week that passed, Jordy dropped off another sketch, each one riskier than its predecessor. Samantha couldn't quite decipher a theme, but Jordy was certainly looking to create new trends. She'd even shared a couple of his designs with a few fashionistas she trusted, all of whom claimed to be excited to see Jordy Theaker working again.

Samantha had to admit that she was disappointed with Jordy's general demeanor. With each design he delivered he was more languid and distraught than before. She could appreciate the artist going to great lengths to tap into his creative force, but at this rate he was going to join the 27 Club. She would have to straighten him out a bit for appearances and interviews. With the work he was producing, he was once again going to be quite a fixture in the fashion world.

As she left the warehouse, she said to her interns, "I'll be back in a little while."

She took a taxi to Jordy's apartment. Knocked on the door but nobody answered.

He didn't live in the best part of town. Couldn't afford to. Just standing in the hallway made Samantha nervous. She couldn't help but think about the possibility that something nefarious had taken place. A drug deal gone wrong, some homophobic thug on rampage.

The door was unlocked. Deciding that Jordy wouldn't mind if she stepped inside for a welfare check, she turned the handle and gently pushed open the door.

"Jordy? Jor—" The smell caught her by surprise.

She probably should have called the police and waited in the hall, but she saw Jordy sitting in a chair across the room and ran to him.

Littered around him were pill bottles, a syringe and a blackened spoon, a small mirror coated with a powdery film. Around his neck was a sign he'd made that said: Live fast, die young, leave an exquisite corpse.

"Jesus."

Something about the odor in the apartment didn't sit well with Samantha. Jordy didn't appear to have been dead for too long. He certainly wasn't decomposing yet. She guessed that he had taken a massive dose of drugs last night, a mix of opiates and speed that his heart couldn't take.

Samantha wasn't aware that she had been looking around the living room until she saw something through an open door down the small hall that led to Jordy's bedroom. A flash of color and something glistening.

She used her cell phone to contact the police. Told them that she dropped by a friend's house and found him dead.

She then walked to the door in the hallway, unable to refuse the macabre pull, because deep down she knew there had to be a reason for the stench. The door was open enough to see something, but she couldn't tell what it was. The color intrigued her, set her senses on fire in the best and worst ways.

The hinge sighed as she pushed the door open.

Samantha caught a scream in her throat as she witnessed the most disturbing and beautiful thing she'd ever seen in her life. It was horrible, revolting ... and the smell!

The body had been dead for weeks. It was crudely fastened to what appeared to be the legs of a circular wooden table. The body hung limp, its rotting flesh slowly dripping onto the floor into small puddles of gore. There was a rod protruding from the wooden base that the corpse was fastened to with wire and rebar. Though the dress, no, gown it wore was exquisite, there were dark patches where the sticky rotting flesh beneath had fused to the fabric.

This was Jordan's masterpiece. This was the piece that would awe the world of fashion.

On the floor in front of the macabre mannequin was a sketch of the gown. The paper was filthy, perhaps dirtied with rot that had transferred onto Jordy's hands while he pinned the gown in place.

There was as knock at the door. Someone said, "Police!"

Samantha grabbed the sketch, folded it and placed it into her purse.

The police found her staring at the macabre beauty that centered the bedroom like something out of Ed Gein's wet dreams. They ushered her into the hallway, assuring her that everything was going to be all right.

She had the design.

Yes, everything certainly was going to be all right.

Beware! The! Beverage!

Jeff Strand

The secret ingredient in Rocketship Energy Drink turned out to be Martian blood. This surprised most of humanity, even though there was a big green alien on the can. The slogan was "It'll power you to Mars!" but still, how could anybody have expected such an odd ingredient in the bestselling beverage on the market?

Originally, the populace of Earth assumed that Rocketship was just another energy drink, like Red Bull or Monster. As with the competition, it was filled with chemicals with names that sounded like vitamins but which the human body did not actually need to function properly. It had a *lot* of sugar even by energy drink standards, which humanity would later learn was necessary because it's extremely difficult to mask the wretched flavor of Martian blood.

"What's that you're drinking?" asked Malcolm, a typical teenager, three months before the horrific secret of Rocketship was revealed to the world.

His best friend Charlie held up the can. "It's the best

thing ever. It's like they sucked the adrenaline out of an Olympic athlete and made it into a carbonated beverage. Honestly, if I had to choose between getting to second base with my lab partner Kim and having a serving of Rocketship, I'd pick Rocketship!"

"You're full of day-old guacamole," said Malcolm. "No way is the drink *that* refreshing."

"Try it."

"Not with your germs all over the can."

"Trust me, if you try this drink, you won't worry about germs ever again!"

With such a passionate endorsement from a close friend he trusted, Malcolm had no choice but to give Rocketship a try. He accepted the can from Charlie and took a great big swig.

It tasted like cough syrup that had been enhanced by about forty-five sugar cubes. It was goooooood. Where had this drink been all his life? Why had he wasted so much valuable liquid ingestion on water, orange juice, and breast milk when he could have been drinking Rocketship?

He wanted to say "This has changed my life!" but he was worried that Charlie might think that was a little weird, so he said "Mmmmm!" instead.

"Good, isn't it?" asked Charlie.

"Can I have the rest?"

"No," said Charlie, reaching for his drink. "You may not."

"Do you have more in the fridge?"

"No."

"Why did you hesitate before you said no?"

"I had to think about it because I couldn't quite remember if there was any in the refrigerator or not. But then I remembered that there wasn't any. It's all gone. Sorry."

"If I look in your fridge right now, are you sure I won't find more cans of Rocketship?"

"You do not have permission to look in there."

"I'm going to check."

"All that's in there is my dad's Rocketship. He'll beat you to death if you take any of his. You know he'll do it. Remember how mad he got that one time we snuck some of his whiskey? Remember? Imagine that times a trillion."

"Then can I have another sip of this one?"

"I'd rather you didn't."

"I'll barely drink any."

"Please return my can to me."

"But the rush of energy is like nothing I've ever encountered!" Charlie had been right—Malcolm was not the least bit concerned about any germs that might have been on the can. He felt like he'd never be sick again! He felt like he could leap over tall buildings! He felt like he could break elephants over his knee! He felt like every single molecule in his body had the strength of six molecules!

"Give me back my Rocketship," said Charlie, narrowing his eyes in a stern manner.

Malcolm felt like he could break somebody's neck—say, for example, Charlie's—and steal his drink.

He could do it.

"How much is this stuff?" Malcolm asked.

"Four bucks a can. You can get it anywhere."

Though Malcolm felt powerful enough to do so, he didn't think it was a good idea to murder his best friend over something that cost four dollars. He had enough money in his wallet to buy two-and-a-half cans without breaking any necks, so that seemed like the better approach.

"I've got to go," he said.

"But we were just about to watch the second movie in the *Lord of the Rings* trilogy again!"

"Sorry. I need my Rocketship."

"That's not cool."

"You can always give me one out of the fridge."

Charlie hesitated. "Do you promise that you'll replace

it?"

"Yes."

"Do you *promise*?"

"I already said yes!"

"Are your fingers crossed?"

"No. We're not six, Charlie. And if crossing fingers was a legally binding loophole in a promise, I could just *say* I crossed my fingers because you would have no way of knowing if my fingers had been crossed or not. So I promise that you don't have to worry about me resorting to six-year-old rules of behavior and trying to escape my debt."

"Do you swear on your mother's life that you'll replace the Rocketship?"

"My mom isn't going to die if I don't keep a promise. That's not the way the Supreme Being does things. If it were, I could swear on Hitler's life and then purposely never replace the drink, just to be rid of Hitler."

"Well, Hitler's been dead for about seven decades."

"I know, but I meant that if somebody in World War II had wanted to kill Hitler, they could swear on his life and then break the promise. I should have used a more contemporary example. But you get my point, right?"

"Swear to me on Hitler's death that you'll replace the can. That way, if you break the promise, Hitler will return from the grave, and you just *know* he'll be up to no good, because Jewish people are still very much with us these days."

"I swear on Hitler's death," said Malcolm. It occurred to him that they were spending a lot of time worrying about a product that would require a ten-minute round trip to obtain. That seemed weird. Why was he so anxious not to be without Rocketship for even a few minutes?

Was it possible that the drink had adverse effects?

Nah. Something that made him feel so energetic could not have a downside. Things that made you feel good were rarely harmful.

Charlie stared at him for a long moment. A very long moment. A moment long enough that Malcolm could have gone out to get the Rocketship and been back. It was actually kind of creepy.

"Okay," Charlie finally said.

He went into the kitchen and returned with an unopened can of Rocketship. It took him another couple of minutes to work up the willpower to hand it over to Malcolm.

Malcolm popped open the top. The enticing aroma made his nostrils sing in a not-literal-but-rather-figurative manner. He took a drink, and once he'd taken that first drink it was a quick progression to the second, and from there he moved rapidly to the third, and then the fourth through twelfth drinks were combined into one long steady gulp.

He finished up the can and crushed it in his hand. He'd had the strength for such a feat before, but today it just felt like a more powerful can crushing.

He let out the mightiest belch of his life and said "I think—"

Charlie punched him in the face, knocking him to the floor.

"Why'd you do that?" Malcolm wailed.

"You said that you thought you were going to refuse to replace the can of Rocketship that you drank!"

"No, I didn't! All I said was 'I think'!"

"And what you thought was that you were going to refuse to replace the can of Rocketship that you drank! You lied to me! And now we'll have the Hitler problem to deal with!"

Malcolm got back up. Energy coursed through his veins. Except for the fact that his face hurt, he'd never felt better in his life.

"*I am the most powerful human being in the world*!" Malcolm shouted at the heavens, raising his arms into the air.

There was an awkward moment of silence.

"Did you really just shout that you're the most powerful human being in the world?" asked Charlie.

"Uh, yeah."

"You're not, you know."

"I feel like I am."

"But you're not. I mean, Rocketship makes me feel good, too, but there are professional athletes who train their entire lives to be in prime physical condition. You're not even top ten. Probably not even top twenty."

"Power doesn't necessarily have to be related to physical prowess."

"So you think you're more powerful than the President of the United States? You think you're more powerful than a mad scientist who has acquired the ingredients to make an atomic bomb? You think you're more powerful than high-ranking employees at Disney? Give me a break."

Malcolm punched Charlie in the face. Not only was the blow powerful enough to break Charlie's neck, but it had sufficient strength to pop his head completely off.

He really hadn't intended to do that. In the future, he'd have to be more careful when he punched somebody.

He'd never seen somebody with a missing head before, and the visual image was unsightly enough that Malcolm almost forgot to take the other cans of Rocketship out of the refrigerator before he left.

On the way out, he accidentally bumped into the mailman. Under normal circumstances, the mailman was totally fine with the occasional accidental bump, as long as the person who'd bumped him offered up a casual apology, but he'd just finished a can of Rocketship and his level of energy was so high that he knew he didn't *have* to be nice about people bumping into him. He punched Malcolm in the face, knocking off his head.

Then he felt bad about it.

And so it began. The world was filled with millions of consumers who had such high energy levels that they could knock people's heads off with a single well-placed punch. Granted, not all of them used their energy for decapitation. There were thousands of recorded incidents of arms being yanked off during handshakes, and people with fist-sized holes in their torsos, and buttocks being kicked completely off.

It was a dangerous time.

Stores couldn't keep Rocketship on the shelves. Almost everybody wanted the rush of energy, and even those who'd turned up their nose and said "I don't drink sugary carbonated beverages" in a snotty manner realized that they needed Rocketship in order to compete.

The world's population decreased by about fifty percent within two weeks. Rocketship also boosted one's libido, so humanity assumed that the population could be replenished, but still, everyone pretty much agreed that the deaths were out of control.

Congress tried to enact legislation banning the beverage, but a sneaky attempt to pass the bill with a clause saying that Rocketship was banned for everybody except members of Congress was noticed by a liberal radio show host, and public outcry was so intense that the government dropped the issue and just asked people to make a reasonable attempt not to knock anybody's head off.

Three months after the tragic demise of Malcolm and Charlie, the population had been reduced to about ten percent of its former quantity. And that's when a scientist discovered the secret ingredient in Rocketship.

"It's Martian blood!" he shouted. "It's Martian blood!"

Because nobody was in the room with him, he hurried out to someplace where other people could hear him shout. "It's Martian blood!" he shouted. "It's Martian blood!"

Humanity was outraged. Nowhere in the ingredients list was "Martian blood" listed.

"This is unacceptable!" said the President of the United States in an address to the nation. "Nobody would drink

Martian blood if they knew beforehand that what they were drinking was Martian blood, and this revelation may very well explain why this drink has cost so many human lives."

The manufacturers of Rocketship insisted that the scientist's findings were untrue. Humanity responded to this denial by getting extremely mad at the scientist, but days later the scientist, who was very ambitious, acquired a video of hundreds of green aliens being squashed in steel machines. Their blood was collected in large tubs, which fed to long tubes, which allocated one drop of Martian blood in each can of Rocketship.

There were a lot of Martians who had not been squashed, and they'd been wondering what happened to their friends, and once this news broke they launched an all-out attack on planet Earth. Unfortunately, though there were only maybe ten earthlings who knew about the Rocketship secret, the Martians blamed everybody without green skin.

The remaining ten percent of humanity dropped down to eight, and then five, and then two. After that, the Martians decided that humanity had learned its lesson and returned to their home planet of Martia.

Though the survivors were sad about what happened to everybody else, it did mean that there was plenty of Rocketship left, so they chugged as much as they wanted. The two percent dropped to one and down to one-half, until only about sixty-three humans remained.

One of them was a serial killer who'd never tried Rocketship, and he knocked the population down to forty.

Then came the flu.

So it was all a great tragedy, except in the life of Milton Tylerson, who was now one of four remaining humans, and the other three were women. He thought things had worked out in a rather awesome manner.

Doctors had told him that he'd never be able to have children, but he kept that information to himself, and lived the rest of his very happy life claiming to be the savior of humanity's future.

Eggbeater

Saul Bailey

My given name's Dale Earle Ray, but I been Eggbeater or Egg for short my whole life, on account of how I's got an eggbeater in place of my cock.

None of my brother's got any malformations of any type, apart from Buck's squint, but the story behind that was he caught a two by four upside the head for whistling at the Gershaw twins outside the store one time. I's too scared to ask him, but it sounds plausible – he did like to whistle at the pretty girls, and them twins was pretty as a picture, back in the day. And they's daddy was a real protective man.

Anyways. So I got eight brothers – Buck, Bob, Huck, Hank, Danny and Donny the twins, Jake and Sammy. I was lucky number nine. After me, mama went and got her tubes tied at that new place that opened up – said nine was enough for any woman, and anyway with how I'd turned out, it was like God was tryin' to tell her somethin' or somethin'.

She said I come out that way. I seen the Polaroid.

Mama holdin' me, little metal thing where my pee-pee shoulda been. The picture hung on the fridge for years, under the Mountain Dew fridge magnet. Thought it was still there, but it ain't. Musta got so used to seein' it, I kept seein' it even after it was gone. Amazin' what the mind can do.

Anyways.

Mama told me we had to keep it secret – said folks wouldn't understand, might make fun, maybe even take me away. I saw how mean the kids were about Joey from the park with his club foot, figured she was right. Of course, my brothers took right on to calling me Eggbeater or just plain old Egg, but lots of folks around these parts got peculiar nicknames, and nobody ever asked me how I came by mine. The whisk grew right along with me, pretty well in proportion. I can pee through it just fine – there's a hole at the end, right in the middle, opens when I need to go and is closed the rest of the time. My nuts are a little odd too, kinda set back and misshapen, but they don't give me no pain, and mama says that's a blessin' and I guess she's right.

She birthed me in the trailer herself, just like all my brothers, so there was no reason for anyone to know, I guess. Anyone outside, I mean. Mama used to joke my daddy must have been a French baker, but I don't think she really knew for sure and I never did either and to be honest I've never really worried about it. Mama raised us all good, and Buck, Bob, Huck, Hank, Danny, Donny, Jake and Sammy all looked out for me too, in their own ways. Taught me how to fight, shoot, fish. Swim too. They all knew about me o'course, but they never said nothin' mean, even when they got to raggin' on me sometimes. It was always my hair or my buck teeth. Never the other. They was good like that, my kin.

Anyways.

We grew up good together. As I got older, though, I started to get problems. I developed young, and around the time I's startin' to get zits and stinky armpits, I started getting strange feelings around baking. Mama never baked at home, but old Lisa-May across the way did. Her old man Dan had a for-real job – he fixed trucks for a living. Went out every day in a uniform and everything, and old Lisa-May'd wave him off and then shut the trailer door, and after a few minutes the sweet smell of baking bread or pie or cakes'd waft out her window.

I mean to say, I'd always liked the smell of baking, I guess – who doesn't? But this summer, I felt it started doing something... peculiar to me. My recollection is the feelings came first, but I couldn't swear to it. Either way, right around then, my Johnson developed in a most alarming manner.

What I mean to say is, a single beater, all I'd ever had and Lord knows all I'd ever needed, had somehow become two. The two sets of blades were interlocked, like them fancy ones you seem the TV chefs use. I mean, overnight this happened.

I didn't know what to do. I'd always worn my pants baggy, but even so this made life awkward. I had to talk to mama about it, and it was so embarrassing havin' to show her, but she was good enough about it, just sighed and said I was God's own private mystery, which she liked to say a lot about me, and then she bought me back sweatpants from the goodwill that were way too big but at least did something to disguise the bulge a bit.

But Lord, the baking became torture! Every time I walked by that open trailer window, I'd smell that fine smell, and feel a painful swelling in my pants. Got so I could barely walk right, would have to go sit in the shade and try and think about other things – for some reason, bicycles'd always do it in the end, just picturing them as clear as I could would make that swelling ease off, get the whisk back down to manageable size.

Still, the situation was becoming intolerable, and finally I realised I was just gonna have to take one big dumb ole risk. So this morning I did: I waited 'till Dan had left for the days work, and I just marched up to Lisa-May's door bold as brass and knocked on the screen door, hard enough to make it rattle.

Lisa-May came to the door, opened it. "Can I help you, sweetheart?" She was a good lookin' woman, Lisa-May, I mean old, you know, maybe thirty or so, but she always took care of herself. She had her long black hair twisted up and held with a pencil, looked like. I could see small black moles on her neck, just a couple. They looked lovely on her pale skin. Had her face fixed up pretty too, just a little makeup, none of what my mother sometimes called 'tramp warpaint'.

I licked my lips, feelin' shy, but spoke up loud and clear. "Well, mam, I was wonderin' if you were plannin' on doing some of your bakin' this fine morning?"

She put her hands on her hips then, rocked back on her feet a little. I could see she was tryin' to take the measure of me. I looked back, at the white tank-top she had on, a little tight around her bazookers, and I realised I could see a black bra underneath. She had a full figure, you know – not fat, but… curvy. Cuddly, I guess. She wore it well, is what I'm tryin' to say.

Anyways.

She looked me up and down, and eventually said 'Why yes I am, young man, but may I ask what business is it of yours?" She said it cool, but not stuck up or angry. I think like she was really curious, you know. So I says, like I practiced, "Well, m'am, I'd really like it if maybe you could teach me how."

There was another long silence. I could see her thinking about it. I felt nervous in case she said no and excited in case she said yes but also I felt calm, somehow, because she seemed kind and I'd asked the way I'd wanted to ask, and I guess that doesn't make much sense but that's how I remember it.

"What's your name, boy?"

"Egg, mam."

"Egg's what they call you. What's your name?"

"I'm Dale Earle Ray, mam."

"And Dale Earle Ray, you want me to teach you how to bake?"

"Yes m'am, I do. I's a quick study." I felt a little flushed at that last – it wasn't strictly speaking a lie, but there's some things I took to quick and some things that never really stuck no matter how long I tried, and I didn't know for sure which baking would be, but I wanted her to teach me so I figured that I'd better just go with it and hope it worked out.

"And why do you want to learn, Dale? You got a girl you want to impress or something?" She smiled then, a real kind smile, and I knew it was gonna be okay, that she'd let me stick around.

"No, m'am. I's hopin' to be able to bake for my mama, learn how to make her bread. Maybe even a cake, for her birthday."

Her smile got wider, showing white teeth. She looked really pretty when she smiled like that. "well Dale Earle Ray, ain't you a sweet young thing? Of course I'll be happy to teach you what I know, ain't nothing to it really. I'm sure you'll pick it up real fast."

I smiled back at that, and I'm pretty sure I was blushing too, sure felt like my face was hot anyways. She stuck the fan on, and said "Come on in" and waved me over to the breakfast bar in the middle of the living room. "Take a stool, hun, I'll just bring over the ingredients." I looked over as she bent to peer in the fridge. Something about the way her behind moved in those white pants did something to me, and I felt things beginning to get a little uncomfortable down there, but luckily I was sat down and had the counter for cover. I turned to look out the window for a distraction, but all the blinds were drawn, like usual. I tried to think about 'cycles instead as the sounds of her rummaging and opening and closing cupboards came from the open kitchen area.

"Now, I hope it's okay, but I was already plannin' on makin' gingerbread men this mornin' – got the ground ginger from the store just yesterday. It's a good place to start anyway, simple enough for you to get a feel for things…" her voice drifted above the sound of ingredients and utensils being assembled.

"..maybe if we have time afterward, we could make some of my Derby Pie. Treat Dan when he gets home. That man does love a slice of pie." She laughed then, and it was like music. Warmed me right up.

She came over to the bar with arms full of ingredients and laid them all out on the table – a small sack of flour, ground ginger in a red-lidded jar, a yellow box with bicarbonate of soda printed on the side, a pack of butter, a bag of sugar, a box of eggs, and a dark red tin of treacle. Then she took out the eggbeater. I stared at it. Twin bladed and threaded, like me, but with a turn handle at the top, unlike me.

I turned my eyes away somehow and saw her take a smaller bowl out of the larger and put a metal sieve on top of it. Then she went back to the kitchen, grabbed a plastic scale and brought it back. "First we gotta sieve the flour" she said, weighing out an amount, then tipping it into the sieve. She showed me how, then I carried on with that while she spooned out some of the ginger and soda and sprinkled it on top. It took a little while to sift the powder but I stayed patient and did like she showed me, trying not to fidget or bend at the belly, even though it felt like I had a small bunny bouncin' around my insides. Every time I caught a glimpse of her beater out the corner of my eye, or the eggs in their pack, I felt a surge in my pants, an ache that just stopped short of really painful.

Eventually, we were done siftin'. "Very good, Dale. Now put that to one side there."

I slid the bowl over the counter, like she asked.

She took the second bowl, the butter and the sugar. I

watched her as she weighed out the sugar, pouring it into the bowl when she was done, then cutting off a lump from the block of butter and tossing it carelessly in on top.

"Now, are you ready to get beating, Dale?"

I didn't trust myself to speak, my throat felt all dried up and I was afraid I'd just squeak, or say nothing at all. The tightness in my belly was making it a little hard to breathe, and I felt sweat runnin' down my face.

"You okay, hun? Are you gettin' too hot?"

I sure was, but it wasn't the warmth of the trailer doin' it. I shifted in my seat, awful uncomfortable, and the blades of my business rubbed together with a muffled clank.

I saw her eyes widen a fraction. She'd heard me.

"What you got under there?"

The way she asked was so kind, so open and unafraid and... I dunno how to say it, but it made me feel safe somehow.

My legs were a little wobbly but I managed to get them under me and stood up. The bulge was huge, even through the baggy sweatpants. I looked down at it, too scared to meet her face, too scared of what I might see.

I heard her breath catch, then come out long and slow.

"You got somethin' in your pocket there, mister?"

Her voice was calm. Not angry, but not exactly friendly anymore either. I shook my head. My face was pounding with my heartbeat. I was sweatin' all over for real.

"What is it?"

I couldn't talk. I mean I tried but I just made this kind of squeak. I was scared and miserable and thought I might just up and die of embarrassment, but that darn thing in my pants was as alive as it'd ever been, so big and dumb. I hated it. Hated myself, for comin' and puttin' myself in this spot, gettin' this nice lady in such a horrible position. What on earth had possessed me?

She took another breath, and this time, when she spoke again, the kind was back in her voice.

"Show me."

My arms moved by themselves, felt like. I hooked the pants, stretching out the waistband to make sure they cleared it, and pulled 'em down. I had my head down too, so I was starin' down at those blades. They pointed up at me, swayin' just a little from the movement, at a slight angle away from my belly.

I just stared and stared, sweatin' and breathin' heavy. I believe I'd still be standing there now if she hadn't put her hand under my chin. I looked up, afraid to meet her eye but unable to look away. She was bent forward, so I got a good peak down her top as I looked up. I felt like I shook a little then but that might just have been inside.

I met her eyes. They were very blue and very sweet. I felt the worst of the panic fade a little – she wasn't screamin', hadn't thrown me out, and now she was looking at me like maybe it was okay.

"Honey... Is this why you came here? Why you wanted to bake?"

I nodded. Held her eyes. Before I couldn't look, now I couldn't look away.

"Did someone do this to you?" So gentle, careful.

I shook my head.

She nodded, tried on a smile. It looked good. "You were brave to come here, Dale. I see that now.. Have you... have they ever moved?"

I really did think I was goin' to faint then, just for a second, but I didn't, I just said "no, ma'am" which came out all shaky, and tried not to start blubbin'.

She smiled wider at that. Well, let's see what we can do about that, shall we?"

Next thing I know, I'm up on the counter, on all fours. She put the mixing bowl under me, then said "go ahead honey" and I lowered myself into the butter and sugar. I could feel it against the blades. It felt amazin' and irritatin' all at once. My tummy was all fluttery.

Nothin' happened. I grit my teeth and willed and

willed, but nothin' moved. Felt like it wanted to, but...

"Honey, do you mind if I take my hands to.. to you here? Just to see if we can get things going?"

I shook my head, glad not to have to look at her. My head was pounding with hot blood. I musta been red, I sure felt red. Excited and scared and wrong and so right, and not quite right, all at once.

Her fingers traced the blades, then up to where the tube met my body. I couldn't help a little shudder, but the blades didn't move.

"Sorry, honey, I'm just tryin'..."

"It's okay, ma'am."

"Well now, I think you can call me Lisa-May now, don't you, given all we've been through?" As she spoke the fingers reached around my shrivelled sack, and suddenly I felt somethin' and my breath caught.

"Oh." She sounded cautious, but also.. I dunno, eager? Interested? Something. She stroked the skin there, then her fingers found a nub of something hard where I guess my balls shoulda been. As soon as her fingers touched it I had to moan.

"Oh." More sure this time. "Honey, I think we've got something here. You want me to...?"

"Yes, please, ma... Lisa-May, please..."

Her fingers tightened on the nub. It moved, and suddenly I felt the blades turn too, rotating together though the butter, slicing it up into the sugar, blendin' them together.

"This feels amazin', m... Lisa-May!"

"You're blendin' 'em real good! Hang on."

She swapped hands then, usin' the other to crack an egg into the mix. I felt the cold slime from the white and yolk mix with the butter and sugar under my spinnin' blades, and it felt so good, makin' this mixture squeeze through 'em, between 'em, and my belly got tighter and tighter as she cracked in the other two eggs, finger workin' that hard nub all the time, and I took to moving my hips around, drivin' the mixture around the bowl, little splashes coming up and coating my thighs. She giggled, a lovely sound, like she could feel my pleasure. Me, I felt like I was doin' what I always shoulda been doin', like the world made sense for the first time I could remember. She finally tipped in the treacle, and revved me up, and man I felt somethin' build and build and then just *go*, like a pullin' that ran up my leg and into my spine, then a pumping feeling right through my blades. I made a noise like "Ggggg!" and the blades just span and span and blended, and I could feel something passin' out of me and into the mix, squirtin', but I couldn't see nothin' and thought maybe I was imagining that part. It was a great feelin', but I noticed they started to slow down a bit after, started shrinkin' back a little, and Lisa-May said, "That's okay honey, you did real good", and she put a towel over the stool and I sat down on it, pants around my ankles, and watched her fold in the flour and make the dough. Watchin' her kneed it out, then roll it flat, and start cuttin' shapes, I felt somethin' stir, and sure enough those droopin' blades were startin' to grow again – it was a little unsteady at first, almost painful, but they were definitely on the rise. She saw it and looked up at me, with a twinkle in her eye, and said "Well, ain't you a healthy young man? Maybe we'll get a second round of something done. Would you like that?"

I nodded, and it made the thing growing out of me nod too, and she laughed. "I swear Dale, it's like we were made for each other, ain't it? Me with my love of the baking and you with your..." She waved at my doin's, looking at them. I liked that. Liked her looking at it. She spoke, talking more to the beater than me, seemed like, but I didn't mind "It's a thing of beauty. I swear. If only..."

I didn't want her to finish that sentence, and she didn't. She looked up instead. 'Well, ain't you a mess?"

I looked down, saw the blades all caked with the dough mix. Bobbing up at me. The splatters on my belly and legs.

I giggled.

"Yes, Lisa-May, I sure am." She laughed too.

"Well, you just hang tight, we're gonna get you cleaned up." She took the gingerbread men over to the oven, put them in, then came back. She squatted in front of me, close, her hands on my shoulders. Her face was serious, but her eye contact made me throb down there worse than ever. Anyways, she didn't seem mad, only serious.

"Now Dale, I don't think you and I have done anything wrong here. Do you?"

I wasn't 100% sure, to be honest, but it sure didn't *feel* wrong, so I shook my head.

"Good. I only ask because I'm now gonna ask you somethin' that might make it seem bad, but it ain't. It's just... I don't think other people would understand. Do you get me?"

I thought about Joey's club foot and all the mean awful thing people said, and I looked down at myself and "Yes ma'am, I get you."

Her hand went under my chin again, gentle but firm. Her eyes seemed a little damp this time, I thought. Or maybe it was mine.

"And I am a married woman. Dan's a good man, an understandin' man, but this... This has to be ours, do you understand? Our secret?"

I nodded, holdin' her eyes to show I was serious. She saw that and smiled again. "You're a creature of beauty, Dale. Anybody ever tell you that?"

"Lisa-May, I think you're about the most beautiful woman in the whole world, and that's the truth."

She giggled and blushed. "Hush, boy. You're very sweet."

She leaned closer. "You will keep this as ours, won't you?"

"I will."

She smiled again, showing teeth, her eyes sparkly again, and it made my belly do a flip. "Now, let's get you cleaned up."

She kneeled down and put her lips to my belly, kissing and licking away the mix. I gasped, feeling her warm there, hot and wet, and I felt the blades go rigid. She used her mouth to clean off all the mix from my thighs and stomach, then she took the metal in her hand and looked up at me. "These things ever move without the touch?"

I shook my head. "Never. They can't."

She smiled. "Good." Then she started licking the blades.

I don't know how long she did it for. I shut my eyes, just rocked by the feeling of her tongue and lips running all over me, then opened them again, wanting to watch. She looked back up at me, then closed her eyes and put her mouth over one blade, then the next, moving her wet tongue over the part in her mouth. The blades were as big and hard as I could ever remember, and I felt like I was going to explode, but they didn't move even a hair as she did what she did.

Eventually she stopped and held her face back. I could feel her breath where the blades were wet with spit. They gleamed. She smiled, then reached her hand up underneath. Her fingers brushed the nub, then squeezed...

I felt that pull in my belly and legs again. The blades spun, and that pumping kicked in. I saw her face get sprayed with spit, then something else that came out the end of the beater, where the pee comes out. She closed her eyes and I watched this stuff spray over her cheeks, nose, and lips, some of it hitting her neck, running down her exposed cleavage.

I just stared as she took another towel and wiped herself down, cleaning the stuff away. I felt great, but also scared. I thought about that stuff gettin' in the mix earlier when I done that before, how it musta done, and I thought about sayin' somethin' about that, but I didn't. Instead, I said

"I didn't know that was gonna..."

She smiled at me, a real smile. "Don't worry honey, I did. Did it feel good?"

I nodded, still a little unsure.

"Good. Me too." She wiped herself down, cleaning off her hands on the towel. "Now pull your pants up."

I did, and then a buzzer went off in the kitchen. "Sounds like the men are ready!" She said, happy, and went to get them out of the oven. I slumped back on the chair, exhausted.

I woke up to the sound of her choking. It was dim and I couldn't see properly at first. I heard the noise, like a cat throwing up, but deeper. I looked around.

I'd fallen asleep on her sofa, and she was over in the easy chair. By the looks, she'd been asleep herself. Her head was thrown back.

Sat on the back of the chair were two of the gingerbread men we'd made, one either side of her head. They had their little arms on her forehead, forcing it back. On her front, I could see four of them climbing up her body, clinging to her clothes as she bucked and rocked. Her arms were pinned by more of them. I looked up at her face. A gingerbread torso was poking out of her mouth, wriggling. The arms were tryin' to push her jaws wider. I could see behind her teeth was just a wall of biscuit, crumbed up and blocking her mouth completely.

I did a count. Two holdin' her head. Two on each arm. Four more climbing up her. One in the mouth. So three of 'em musta already been blocking her throat.

The thought got me moving for some reason. I leapt up and brought my fist down on the one holding her left hand. They musta been strong, but I guess they was still made outta gingerbread, because he damn near exploded in a shower of crumbs. Her freed hand went straight up to her face, but just grabbed at her throat, as if she could clear it from the outside.

The others never reacted to me, and I crushed them all in turn, grabbing the ones off her body and stomping them into ginger dust, but by the time I'd finished and tried to clear her throat, she'd already passed. I phoned the ambulance and I guess they phoned the police and they took me here and now I'm talking to you, and I know the story sounds crazy and I'm sorry about what happened to Lisa-May but the proof is right here in my pants and you'd better call the people who are still in the trailer, because we made a Derby Pie after and it was still in the oven when I got taken out and I don't want to think about what *that's* gonna do when it's done baking.

Please Subscribe

Adam Cesare

Uploaded 1 Month Ago

"Hey guys. Melody here, and this is my first of what I hope to be many videos."

We're in a typical webcam medium shot.

The girl on screen is attractive but not the most attractive we've seen.

And that's okay, because she's got stiff competition. We do watch *a lot* of videos. And once she watches a few more, herself—some tutorials on proper lighting (the difference between key and fill), a couple of make-up how-tos—then maybe she will rank among the most beautiful.

"I'm new to this whole thing, but I see that the surefire way to get likes and subscribers is to live-stream myself playing video games. But, and I hate to break this to you, Internet, but: I'm not a gamer. Unless phone games count.

"No. My content is going to be..."

She scrunches up her nose in a way that can only be

described as self-aware. It's a calculated movement. Calculated, but we are all in agreement that the nose-scrunch is undeniably *adorable*.

Yes, her first video isn't of the highest quality, but this is a girl who knows what she's doing. This channel will get more interesting. It's definitely worth sticking around for the remaining two minutes and thirty-four seconds of her first video.

"Well, I actually don't know what the content on my channel is going to be. And I'm hoping that maybe you guys could help me decide. Leave me a comment and slap a like on this video to help me get some views. But, before you leave, let me tell you a little bit about myself."

She begins a list, counting off her attributes on her fingers like she's only got the ten.

The list goes:

She's eighteen.

She doesn't say where she's living now, but she'll be attending Rutgers in the Fall. That gives us a general location, if she's going away for college but not too far away.

Melody Bliss, her channel name, isn't her real name. No duh!

Her interests include music (classical music, actually, she was first chair violin in high school and hopes to continue the instrument in college), volleyball, and watching bad TV with her friends. And that's not an editorializing on our part, she actually calls it "bad TV", which is a level of self-reflection that many young women do not possess. Especially young women who post cell phone videos of themselves online.

She has two dogs. Which is boring.

But she also has a hermit crab that she got at the boardwalk two years ago. She seems proud she's been able to keep him alive this long. "He's molted three times!" she tells us. We're not sure what that means, but her enthusiasm is quirky and adorable (that word again) and already on-brand.

But there's a big clue in that hermit crab discussion, because she called going to the beach going "down the shore." That means we've successfully triangulated her to the tri-state area. Probably Philly or South Jersey.

Melody signs off—as most of them do—with a plea to subscribe to her channel.

So we subscribe.

Uploaded 3 Weeks Ago

"Hey guys. Did you miss me?"

She's back. Very few young vloggers stick to a schedule. Some never even make a second video, forgetting about that silly dream of internet stardom after their first video fails to break fifty views.

But *this girl*. She's got moxie. We're all in agreement there.

Moxie and a black eye. She's tried to hide the injury with concealer, but she must not have watched a tutorial on that, either: the bruise is glaringly apparent.

Whatever happened to her eye must have happened not long after she recorded her last video, because the mark has already begun to heal. There's a thin crescent of discoloration against the bridge of her nose that's brownish instead of a dark, attractive purple.

Her makeup technique is no better, but she's learned some video production tricks.

This video has a custom thumbnail. Also the lighting and framing is worlds better.

This is *quality content*.

"So I got a few responses to the last video, some comments, and I thought I'd go through and address some of them."

We all lean a little bit closer to our screens at hearing this. It doesn't matter the size of the screen, even if we're watching on a phone and could more easily lift the screen closer to us, we *still* lean forward.

Because maybe she's going to address our questions directly.

Maybe she's going to say our name.

"The request I received the most was if I could play you all something on my violin. And maaaaaybe I will if we can get my page to 100 subscribers by next week, but I don't think I'm feeling up to it today."

She touches the side of her face with the bruise, but doesn't address it directly.

Melody: you're holding out on us.

How did you hurt your eye?

We all want to know.

"And then there were some comments that were..." she pauses, searching for the words in, by this point, her trademark, cutie-pie way. "Let's call them rude."

She looks deeper into the camera.

"I had to delete many of them. Sorry, pervs! This is a family show."

She smiles, changing the subject, switching gears with an almost audible click as her smile brightens.

"There was one other common viewer request that I think I can give you all the hook up with."

She reaches both hands under the frame and our collective hearts leap because not only can we see a little further down her shirt, but she comes back up holding...

A fish tank?

An empty fish tank, with a fog of condensation on the sides and cling wrap over the lid.

"You all wanted to meet Pablo the hermit crab. And he wants to meet you!"

She removes the lid, lifts out a pathetic little creature in an oversized shell. She places Pablo flat on one hand. A few seconds elapse as she waits silently for him to poke his antennae under his shell. He tastes the air, then pops his eye stalks and legs out and makes a beeline for the edge of her hand.

"Nope. Yer not allowed to play outside of your cage, buddy." She says, not to us but to the small land crab.

"Well, that's Pablo. I feed him pellet food I order online, mostly. But occasionally I'll chop him up some fresh vegetables or give him some peanut butter. But that's just on special occasions. Right, Pablo?"

"Si." she says, in Pablo's voice. The choice of language and accent, coming from this white girl, is… problematic. Then she drops the little critter back into his cage.

"If you all want to get your own crabs, I've linked some good care instructions down in the description. Be sure to check those out, because there's a lot more to taking care of hermies than just the wire cage they give you at the beach."

Deep breath. Here comes the plea.

"If you want to see more of me or Pablo, please like this video, then hit the subscribe button. I'll see you here next week and maybe even play you a song, if we hit our goal. Remember: I'm still not sure what this whole thing is, so any suggestions are appreciated."

We hit like.

Then we prepare our comments.

Uploaded Two Weeks Ago

Melody doesn't say anything to kick off her latest video. There's ten seconds of silence, her staring at the camera with her mouth closed around something.

The pose is like she's holding her breath under water, puffing her cheeks out.

The bruise is still there. Barely. But still there, some slight discoloration that only serves to make Melody look tired, not battered.

Then she opens her mouth and Pablo crawls out over

her tongue and plops into her waiting hands.

In Melody's much-improved lighting, his shell glistens. But other than the sheen of spit, Pablo seems none the worse for wear. He cleans off one antenna with his smaller front claw.

Then Melody begins laughing, an embarrassed but unrestrained outpouring of "can you believe I just did that?"

Coming from many other YouTubers, the laughter would read as self-conscious and cloying. But on Melody it's endearing.

"I watched a video that explains you have fifteen to twenty seconds to capture your audience's attention."

She holds Pablo up to the camera so we can see that, yes, he is indeed okay. Maybe a little bewildered. But it's hard to read any emotion in his tiny black eyes.

"Do I have your attention?"

Yes she does.

The video then cuts to a bumper. It's a simple fading in and out of Melody's name, but when we cut back to her, there's also an annotation that pops up on the side of the screen imploring us to subscribe. She has come so far, so fast. Learned so much.

Without her cheeks puffed out to hold her pet inside her mouth, it's becoming apparent that Melody has lost some weight since posting her first video, two weeks ago. She doesn't mention it, but we can see that the line where her neck meets her chin is a little sharper.

Her cheeks are less full, but it looks good on her, accentuates the dimple on her left side. You could lose a penny in that thing.

We all sigh when she smiles wide enough to flash the dimple. We like her better this way. We'll tell her so in the comments.

"I'm sure many of you know by now, but we did reach our subscriber goal, so I'm going to play you a song at the end of this video, but first I wanted to put a question out there: what are your essential dorm room items? I, like, just this morning found out that I'm going to be in freshman housing, in a double, which means that I'm going to have a roommate. I hope she's cool. So, on my list I've already got Christmas lights, collapsible hamper, and flip flops—for the showers."

She exhales, inhales. She's getting better at talking to the camera, but still needs to work on pacing. "But I'm sure that there's a ton of stuff I'm not thinking of. Leave me a list! Give me some life-hacks!"

We can all think of a few suggestions.

We take our eyes off Melody for a moment and look around the frame at what else we can see in her bedroom. There's a pile of laundry that she maybe doesn't realize the camera's picked up, because on top of that pile is a little pink bra.

"Moving on," she says, leaving a slightly awkward pause in instead of editing it out, as she seems to have done in her previous two uploads, which are so tight.

She's not getting lazy. She's just allowing herself to appear more human, less processed. We approve.

"A few of you had noticed that I have a black eye and wanted to know what happened. I guess I'm not as good with makeup as I thought. Or you're all very perceptive [dimple smile]. But no, nothing scandalous. That's just what happens sometimes on the court. The volleyball court. I'm not like, being abused or anything. My videos aren't a cry for help or something. Just want to reach out."

Then there is an edit, no pause, and in the next set-up, more zoomed out, Melody has her violin resting under her chin.

"I read somewhere that videos over six minutes don't do well. So this is going to have to be a quick song," she says and begins to play, beginning with a downstroke, a deep sound. There's a little bit of echo in her bedroom, but she has the camera far enough from the instrument that there's no feedback.

We alternate between watching her hands as she plays and watching that pink bra.

She's quite talented. The song isn't mopey, but it's not joyous either. It's neutral, fast without being particularly invigorating.

"That's all for this week," she says, ending mid-song, it would seem. She tells us to like and subscribe and share.

We are left wanting more.

Uploaded a Week Ago

"A knife, garbage bags (the heavy-duty kind), condoms (all sizes), a shovel," she says, reading off a list.

"You guys are hilarious, but those aren't the kind of dorm room supplies I was talking about."

God, between this week and last week she must've lost fifteen pounds.

The bumper cuts back in after she's done talking. She's got this "starting with a hook" thing down to a science. Who wouldn't want to keep watching?

Not us.

She's rearranged her bedroom. We can no longer see the pile of clothes. Or the bra. She's moved a bookshelf to the edge of her desk and put Pablo's cage on top of the shelf, so we can see him in there, clinging to a knotted length of driftwood.

"Got a lot of comments on last week's video. Also got a lot of hate for my trick with Pablo. Some people called it animal cruelty. Some called it just plain gross. But you know what I say?"

No, what do you say?

"Eff the haters! Efff them right in the ear!"

It's like she can hear our applause from the other side of time and the internet, because she pauses to let her bold stand against "teh haterz" sit for a moment.

Yeah. Eff them. Eff those fucking fucks.

"But those people are in the minority. So thanks to all my *viewers* who left me comments of support. And for those of you looking for me to do something bigger and crazier... all I have to say is stay tuned."

She almost, almost, said 'fans' instead of viewers. The hesitation was microscopic. But we all felt it.

We detected that wriggling diva larvae. The diva that we've planted deep inside the base of Melody's skull. The diva seed.

She longs to call us her *fans*, wants us to tear at the hem of her garment, wants us to tear each other apart but she won't get it. Not yet. As of this video, we are a united front.

There's been no indication as to what the content of this video will be and there's less than a minute left to it. Hardly time for another song or stupid pet trick. What are you going to show us Melody? Is this even a full episode? A measly two minutes is supposed to be our weekly fix?

We are unimpressed.

"Today I..."

"Today I..."

It's like she's stuck, but then we notice the drip that streaks down below her left nostril. There's a watery red line drawn above her lip. She's gotten a nose bleed but she doesn't cut the camera. Instead she covers it with one bent finger, trying to stopper the nostril with a knuckle, and keeps talking.

"That's all the time I've got for today, check back soon for something really spectacular, keep those comments coming in and make sure that you like and subscribe, if you haven't already."

Before the video ends she gives us viewers a quick wave, not with her free hand but with the one she's been using to staunch the blood.

The flow has trickled down, from the knuckle of her pointer finger down so that it drips off the end of her pinky. It's like she's made of marble and in the middle of a

Roman Fountain, the water pumping from her a dark red.

Her wave is such a quick motion that the blood forms a fan. The video cuts off right when the spatter peppers the side of her desk, the bookshelf and Pablo's tank.

Getting only a two minute video seemed like a rip-off at first. But we've watched it, collectively, 5,000 times by this point, a mere three hours after it was uploaded.

We pay special attention to that last twenty seconds, trying to map out where all the droplets of Melody Bliss will fall.

Uploaded Just Now

We're beginning to suspect Melody may have an eating disorder.

Or suspect that she takes comments on the internet way too seriously.

We feel that she's done what she swore she would never do. She's let the haterz get the better of her.

Ironically, she's grown an immense audience in a short amount of time. We hope that she knows that this type of success is atypical. We've never seen anything quite like it. It's not like she has millions of views. She hasn't gone viral. But it's fair to say that she's got a cult audience.

No, that's not a pun.

At the start of this video—freshly uploaded but we all get to it at the same time because we've all set up to be sent email alerts whenever Melody Bliss posts a new video—we're all praying that she gets help. Maybe once she gets to Rutgers, visits their dining hall, she'll put on the freshman fifteen and all will be right with the world.

If she pulls out of this tailspin then we'll have her to internet adore and internet whisper to for many years to come.

We'll be with her when she gets a lucrative sponsorship deal or writes a coffee table book or marries a

Hollywood star who's *actually famous*.

But then she speaks for the first time in this video and it seems pretty clear that none of those things will come to pass.

"Hey guys, Melody here. Just a quick video I made about something I've been getting asked about and have wanted to talk about." Her speech is halting, labored even. She's not annoyed, just tired and unable to concentrate on the words that she's so clearly reading off her computer monitor. They aren't good words.

We'd be able to tell she was reading from the slight, tennis-match back and forth of her eyes, but then she makes it more obvious by squinting at a few words.

"First, I want to say that I appreciate those of you who've reached out to ask if I'm sick," she coughs, in bold defiance of what she's about to say: "No. I am not ill, and I am not sick in the head, either. I *do not* have an eating disorder, but I *have* been on a diet."

She swallows hard, gets wistful. "Summer used to be such a fun time, but I guess this is what growing up's about because I'm so..." she searches for the word, she's either going off-book or she's lost her place.

"Stressed. I've become stressed. I mean, I used to worry about tests, but when I asked for dorm room tips and got to talking to some of you about your college experiences, it got me caught in a kind of cycle."

We don't notice it until now, but the lid is off Pablo's cage and he doesn't appear to be inside.

"I spend all day worrying about every little detail. The future is terrifying y'all."

That last bit isn't a southern-ism, it's more of a youthful borrowing of urban slang. And it feels like it's meant as a joke, but we aren't laughing.

Oh, Melody. We really *did* believe in you.

Maybe it's not too late, we all think, nearly at the same time, all across the country, the English-speaking globe, really, because Melody even has a small but fierce following in Germany. Who knew? Not Melody, because she doesn't seem to know how to check her analytics, at least she hasn't given any indication that she does.

It's not too late if we all go into the comments, right now, even before this video is finished, and we all write *one nice thing*.

One thing about Melody that makes us happy. Makes us proud to be a part of her community, her subscribers and, yes, her fans.

You're the best Melody.

OMG. Hair's so cute today!

There's some kind of *sound*. We're missing action as we type but we must press submit on our new comments.

More Pablo! Love him!

The *sound* again.

You need closet organizers! They're lifesavers in a dorm.

The *sound* is a smack.

Can you shoot a vid showing how you do your make-up?

Fuck you. Kill yourself, slut.

Oh, we all recoil at the dingus among us who felt the need to write that last comment. We bristle as a collective organism.

But a few bad apples...

By the time we all scroll back up after typing out our positivity, Pablo's on screen.

Cute little Pablo! If Melody keeps making videos, one of us is going to have to make Pablo his own Twitter account where "he" can share cute memes and aphorisms. We wouldn't want any money in exchange for doing something like that. We'd just want Melody to acknowledge what a nice gesture it is.

Pablo looks troubled, he's crawling across the desk, searching out a place to hide.

And he finds it in Melody's hair. Her chestnut curls are so wide and well-kept that Pablo is able to use one of them as an impromptu cave.

Melody's hair has fallen across her desk, pushed her keyboard away, apparently bumping the camera to a lower vantage.

She's performed a literal headdesk.

But it's only once the blood begins to spread, the salty blackness of it chasing Pablo out of his hiding spot so he slips off the desk—we hope to land unharmed on the carpet—that we realize that those smacks we heard were repeated headdesks.

Putting her face down onto the desk and into a kitchen knife that Melody has held horizontally (not vertically, like would make more sense). The flat of the blade is flush with the particle board of her Ikea desk. The sharp part is embedded in Melody's forehead.

It's sad. And she's unresponsive, but the thing we all marvel at is: How did she manage to get this video uploaded? There must be a program or function for it that we've never heard of. Maybe a Google Chrome extension?

Amazing. Melody went from a nobody to a seasoned expert in less than one month.

Oh well. There's nothing more for us to see here, the video is over, the pool of blood from the gashes in her skull spread as far as it's going to go.

The video ends.

We unsubscribe.

Abstinence

Shane McKenzie

"What are the rules?"

Vanessa shrugged. "Don't know what counts and what doesn't. I mean…I know you're not supposed to put it, you know, inside of me. Here." She pointed to the zipper of her jean shorts, felt her face burn red. "But what about other places?"

"Like what?"

"You know. Openings."

"Openings?"

"Holes. I don't think you're allowed to put it in any holes at all. Or it counts as…"

An awkward silence hung in the air long enough that Vanessa thought about just forgetting the whole thing. The vibrations in her groin kept her in the closet with him. Her eyes rose from the floor to Brent's groin. She didn't mean to stare. Her eyes were supposed to keep elevating until meeting his gaze, but when she saw the bulge, when she made out the shape of the tip, her eyes refused to budge.

Brent stepped toward her, reached out, but stopped,

let his hand fall back to hanging at his side. "Maybe we shouldn't touch each other. If we don't touch each other, it can't count. No matter what we do, it can't count. Right?"

Vanessa scratched behind her ear. "But if we don't touch each other…what's the point?"

"Right. Maybe we can touch each other, but we just don't touch…you know. Down there."

She still didn't see the point, but nodded anyway.

He took another step toward her, hugged her, but stuck his butt out so his bulge couldn't make contact with her. She almost reached out and touched it, but stopped herself. If that was the one rule, she was going to follow it.

They kissed. Long and hard. Both holding their groins uncomfortably away from each other like two dogs they were trying to keep from fighting. Brent's hand slid up her stomach, paused, then cupped her left breast. Her heart was beating so fast and strong she thought it would rip her shirt and break the bones in his palm.

"This okay?" he asked, the whispery words flowing into her mouth.

She nodded as she swallowed them down. Let him squeeze her breast for a few minutes before becoming impatient and pulling her T-shirt over her head. She hoped he'd get the idea and unclasp her bra, but he didn't. Just went back to cupping and squeezing and kissing.

She couldn't blame him. He had never done anything like this before. When he told her that a few months back, she didn't believe him. How could a boy like Brent be so…innocent? She knew now that he had been telling the truth. She had no more experience than he did, but had seen plenty of steamy scenes in R-rated movies to know what to do. Did a little research on the internet which taught her more about sex than anything she'd been told in school or church.

It was up to her to take charge, she knew that now. So she pulled her bra off, tossed it over her shoulder. His bulge looked painful, pressing up against his jeans. She understood the saying about having a gun in your pocket now. Brent's gun, if the shape was any indication, was a bazooka.

"Vanessa," he said as he ogled her chest, licked his lips. "Are you…are you sure about this?"

"This doesn't count, remember?"

"Right. Can I…touch them?"

She almost rolled her eyes, but forced herself to smile instead as she nodded.

She let him play with them for a good ten minutes. Bouncing them, squeezing them so the fat bulged between his fingers. Pinching her nipples. She reached out, grabbed the back of his head, and pulled him in. Used her left nipple like a crowbar to pry his lips open. And he sucked. He sucked hard enough to cause pain, but she didn't stop him. The pain was strangely nice. She wanted more. Wanted him to bite, but held that back. Didn't want to come on too strong. Not at first. Not while they still had rules.

"Now you," she said.

"Me what?" His eyes were half-lidded as if her breasts had been extracting whiskey.

"Your shirt."

"Yeah. Right."

He started to pull it off, but she stopped him. Wanted to do it herself. She had seen Brent with his shirt off only once. Playing basketball with some of the other boys in the church yard. A hot day. She still remembered the way the sunlight kissed his glistening torso, made the sweat look like spilled orange juice across his chest and belly.

She pulled his shirt off, let her fingers glide across his skin. When she sucked on his nipple, he giggled and flinched away from her.

"What? You don't like it?"

"It tickles too much. What about…what about here instead?"

He turned his head and brushed the side of his neck with his knuckles.

When they had decided to do this, to meet up and experiment with each other, the hardest part was finding a place to go. Either of their houses were a definite impossibility. Just the idea of their parents walking in and catching them made the whole thing seem not worth it. Couldn't go to a public place either in fear of being seen, and neither of them had a car. Brent had brought up the woods, said they could find a nice clearing somewhere, but for whatever reason, that felt too dirty to Vanessa. When she thought of people fornicating in the woods, she thought of prostitutes and rapists, not good Christians like the two of them.

The church was the only answer. The youth center. There were people there every day, but Vanessa knew that Tuesday would be the best time. She scouted it out the week before, searching for the perfect room. Though the maintenance closet was cramped, she figured there was enough room inside. No windows. Only one door. And plenty of supplies if they needed to clean up afterward.

She didn't think about how dark it would be in there, though. Once inside, Brent turned on his cell phone and they used the light from the display screen to see each other. Set it on the floor between their feet so the light was pointed up at them. It made Vanessa think of the Devil watching them, his demonic eyes illuminating their sins. For some reason, the thought made her all the more excited. The screen was too dim to light the entire closet, but bright enough that they could see all of each other. They could almost forget they were in the maintenance closet, but once Vanessa pulled Brent to the ground, they were reminded as supplies were knocked around. A metal bucket dropped to its side, made a sound loud enough that she was sure someone heard it. They paused momentarily, waiting, but nobody came.

She kissed him on the side of the neck like he wanted.

Flicked her tongue across his ear. He gasped, his hands gripping her. One on her thigh, dangerously close to breaking the rule, and the other on her breast.

As much fun as all this was, Vanessa wanted more. Couldn't keep her eyes off his bulge. And when he went back to sucking on her nipples, she reached out and touched it. Gave it a squeeze like you would a clown nose to make it honk.

He flinched away, slapped her hand. "What are you doing?"

"You didn't like it?"

"Of course I… What about the rule?" He had his back pressed against some brooms and mops, his chest heaving, sweat beads forming on his forehead.

"Your jeans were in the way. I didn't really touch you, did I? I just touched your jeans."

He frowned, stared at the floor as he thought about it. "Still doesn't seem like we should be doing that. You can still…you know, feel me. In your hand."

She sighed, used her forearm to cover her breasts. Brent's eyebrows went up and he exhaled like he missed them already.

"What are we doing?"

"What do you mean? We're…loving each other. Aren't we?"

"We never said anything about love."

"I just figured since you invited me to do…this, that's what you meant. That you loved me. You don't?"

"Do you love me?"

His eyes went straight to her breasts. "Yeah. I think so."

"Think so?"

"I made a promise I wouldn't have sex until I was married. Same as you. But here we are, right? That has to mean something, don't you think?"

She let her arm drop and smiled at the look of relief on his face. "I love you."

"I love you."

They kissed again. When he shifted his body to face her, he winced, grunted, and grabbed his bulge. Rubbed it a little. Watching him touch himself like that made Vanessa's heart beat faster.

"What is it?"

"Don't know. Hurts. Bad." He straightened his jeans, gasped again. His eyes widened. "You don't think…you know. Like it's punishment or something, do you?"

"Punishment?"

"God. Punishing me for what we're doing."

"It hurts that bad?"

He gave her a look that answered her question.

"Take it out."

"What? God's mad enough, don't you think?"

"It's not God, Brent. We didn't do anything."

"You touched it. And I've been, you know…sucking on you."

"It's not God. Maybe your jeans are too tight. Just take it out so it has some room."

He thought about it for a second, then stood up. Vanessa thought he was going to leave, but he unzipped his jeans instead, let them drop to his ankles. He kicked his shoes off, his jeans, then hesitated with his underwear before finally yanking them down, too.

His erection, red and long, exploded out from the fabric and wobbled like God's finger, telling them they were doing a bad thing. But the longer she stared at it, the more she was sure there was nothing bad about what they were doing.

"It doesn't look hurt to me," she said.

"It's not that, it's…balls. It's my balls that hurt. Like they're twisted or something."

She scooted closer. Close enough that she could smell the soap he used to wash himself that morning. Close enough that she could see the small slit at the tip of his erection, glistening like he'd applied lip gloss to the edges.

He tried to back away from her, but there was nowhere to go. A bottle of hand soap and a pile of clean rags fell from a shelf and landed right beside her. One of the rags fell across his erection, hung there and made it look like it had floppy bunny ears.

"How do they look? Are they knotted up or something?" His head was turned away, eyes closed, and he spoke through clenched teeth.

"Looks good." She licked her lips.

"You sure?"

"Positive. Maybe they're full of tension, you know? Maybe I can help."

"How can you—"

She grabbed both sides of the hanging towel, wrapped it around one more time, then gently pulled it toward her. As the towel slid down his length, he inhaled sharply, stood up on his tiptoes.

"Vanessa…you-you can't…"

"I'm not touching you. Can't feel anything in my hand except for a towel. Not against the rule, is it?"

She held the towel like a pair of nunchucks. Pulling it tight so the fabric had a strong grip on him. Then slid it slowly back down until she reached the bush of brown pubic hair, pulled it back toward her, back down again.

He wasn't resisting anymore. Wasn't protesting. Just watched her, his breathing growing more rapid as she went faster and faster.

The flesh started to get redder, even more so than it already was. She realized the rough surface of the towel was probably sanding away layers of skin as she went, so she lifted the hand soap bottle from the floor, gave it a strong squeeze and splashed the pink liquid over the entire erection, making sure she hit every spot. He hissed when she did this, stood up taller again, but when she got back to moving that towel, he lowered himself, bit his lower lip.

"Do you like it?"

He nodded.

"Do you love me?"

"Something's h-happening."

"What?"

"It's…something's coming…"

She knew what he meant. Had seen it on the internet. She didn't want to leave any evidence of what they had done that day, so she quickly searched the closet, found a small stack of Dixie cups.

"V-Vanessa…?"

She rose up on her knees, held the cup at the tip. "Go ahead."

It came out in spurts. Like peppermint toothpaste. White and thick.

Brent grunted with every squirt, knocking over more supplies as he scrambled to find something to hold onto. His frantic motion almost made Vanessa miss with her cup, but she managed to catch it. His last spurt hit the edge of the cup, and though most of it still slid in, a few droplets splashed into her face. One on her bottom lip, and the way she saw the girls do on the internet during her research, she stuck her tongue out and licked it up.

Brent smiled, wiped the sweat from his face. She loved that she could make him smile that way. She stared into the cup that was more than halfway filled. Looked him in the eye and smiled.

Then she tilted her head back and drank it. Every drop. Just like the internet told her to do.

The taste, and the consistency, made her gag once, but she swallowed it all down, wiped her mouth, and immediately started pulling her panties off.

"What are you doing?" he said, still staring at the empty cup in her hand with unblinking eyes.

She thought she might need to rub some of the hand soap into herself, but after checking with her middle finger, it wouldn't be necessary. She reached behind her head, grabbed the mop handle, and handed it to him.

"I love you," she said. "Now it's my turn."

The Androgyne

Brendan Vidito

Haden and Daphne entered the motel room and dropped their luggage on the floor.

The place was pregnant with a septic-smelling darkness. Curtains were drawn over the window, and the carpet resembled a fungus the color of bad meat. There were two double beds and a long dresser decorated with thick, yellowed candles. Haden recognized it for what it was: a sacrificial altar.

Daphne inhaled a trembling breath. She moved toward the nearest bed. Haden assisted their shared movement by commanding his legs into motion. They sat down together, as one.

Their flesh was fused at the hip.

Haden's pale flank blended with Daphne's olive-hued skin, meeting in the middle to form a tone unique to their pairing. Their clothes had been specially tailored to accommodate this conjunction of bodies.

They had not always been this way. The unification began shortly after their one-year anniversary. By that time,

Haden and Daphne were together almost every waking hour. Friendships fell to the wayside as they focused on honing their relationship.

Driving home from the movies on a Saturday night, the couple was overtaken by a lustful desire for the other's flesh. They found a secluded roundabout fringed by a forest so thickly leaved it seemed a wall of pure darkness. They clambered to the back seat, dirtying the upholstery with their shoes, and sprawled in a tangle of limbs. Daphne hiked up her skirt and tore a hole in the crotch of her pantyhose. Haden dropped his pants so they hung around his knees. He pulled the crotch of her underwear aside and entered her. The smell of her cunt was like an opiate, clearing Haden's head and filling him with an animal hunger.

They fucked passionately as moonlight trickled through the window, painting their bodies with delicate strokes of white and silver. It made the sweat and cum glittering on their skin look like droplets of a deadly, mercurial poison. As they thrust and grappled, they appeared to become a single organism writhing in death spasm.

When it was over, and they lay together bathed in a hot stew of sex, Daphne let out a shriek of pain and surprise. She looked down between them, where their hips rested side by side. A pale cartilaginous hook had emerged from Haden's skin and was now attempting to pierce her own. The muscles on Haden's hip quivered and swelled, pushing the hook deeper into Daphne. She struggled briefly, taken by a whim of panic, and then Haden placed his hand on her cheek. She calmed down almost instantly. "It's okay, babe," he said. "This is what we want."

She nodded, smiled. The hook sank deeper with a wet fleshy sound. "I love you," she said. He said it back. Their lips pressed together as the hook settled into place with a spastic twitch that reminded them both of an insect. Over the next few months, their flesh adhered around the hook, melding together as one.

Back in the motel room, Haden said, "The sooner we do this, the easier it'll be on the both of us."

He went to stand up, but Daphne wasn't moving. He looked at her and his mind abruptly ceased to recognize reality as a moving sequence of events. Instead, Daphne's movements slowed down, constituting a series of still-lives. Loose strands of her auburn hair were plastered to a freckled brow. Her lips were parted slightly, showing the white of her teeth—arranged to near-perfection by a two-year stint in braces. Her eyes looked toward the altar, the delicate wisp of her lashes framing eyes that were iridescent and flecked with various shades of blue like a living ocean. Once Haden took in every conceivable detail, the still life shuttered and reeled back into motion. Why did it have to come to this? he thought. Why couldn't we just love each other?

"Are you ready, Daphne?"

She wouldn't look at him. "The stuff is in the red duffle."

They stood up together and walked toward the door where they left their bags. After two years of being attached, their shared movement was natural, effortless. They bent down. Haden lifted the red duffle off the floor, and they returned to sit on the bed. Artifacts from their relationship were piled haphazardly inside: the teddy bears they made to resemble one another, photo albums, concert and movie tickets, love letters, handcuffs, jewelry, and sex toys.

They approached the altar and placed each item reverently on the unfinished wooden surface. When the duffle was empty, Daphne hesitated and wrung her fingers together as if trying to mend an invisible object. Then she heaved a lung-emptying sigh and pulled the promise ring off her right ring finger.

Haden watched silently as she placed it among the other artifacts. It met the wood with a dull, inconsequential tap.

Haden opened the duffle's side pocket, pulled out a matchbook and box cutter.

"What is that for?" Daphne said, pointing at the box cutter. Her surprise was audible.

"The Curator said we might need it."

He struck a match and lit each of the five candles.

"Anything else the Curator said that you want to share?" Daphne said with venom.

He had spoken to each of them individually before giving them the key to their room.

"That's all. What did he say to you?"

Daphne hesitated. "That this place is haunted, but not in the way we were conditioned to understand."

Haden shook his head, bewildered. "Whatever the fuck that means."

They sat back down on the bed, simultaneously aware of the next step in the ritual. They had to repeat the act of union that connected their bodies in the first place.

Haden moved his hand to the small of Daphne's back. He used the other to reach over her as he leaned in for a kiss. She was reluctant at first, her lips stiff and unresponsive, but the longer Haden persisted in his affections, the more willing she became. Her lips opened to him, the pink of her tongue darting wet and slick into his mouth. Haden wrapped her in his arms and together they sank down into the mattress.

His lips moved to her chin, brushing the dip beneath her jaw, to her neck where he gently sucked the prickling skin.

He felt the rumble of her vocal cords against his mouth. Daphne said. "How much longer do we have to do this?"

Haden looked her in the eye, saw the pain there, and said, "I don't know."

He knew his answer wasn't satisfactory. The implication of Daphne's words struck him like a blow. By all rights, this *was* torture. They had come to this hole in the wall to breakup, to sever themselves from one another. This ritual seemed like somebody's idea of a sick joke. Laying out their shit like a sideshow, summoning their final dregs of passion in a cruel act of ceremony.

Haden's grip was tight around Daphne's throat as he pressed his mouth against hers, smothering her, his tongue thrusting deeply. Her lips trembled against his. A tear escaped the corner of her eye and glided down her cheekbone.

That kiss held all the pain and finality of a kiss goodbye.

Haden pulled the sundress over Daphne's head, squeezed her breasts and closed his mouth around each nipple until they were engorged and erect. Daphne grappled frantically with the hem of Haden's t-shirt until he got impatient, wrenched it off and tossed it on the floor. When they lay naked, their bodies sheened in the day's sweat, Haden felt Daphne's warmth envelop him. He sighed like a man lowering into a warm bath.

They tasted each other, the salt of sweat on skin, the faint tang of semen, and the warm bitterness of vaginal lubrication. Their fluid mingled in a singular concoction and they drank deeply, a final act of communion. The last feast arranged on a table of clammy flesh, goblets rimmed with enamel or labial tissue, and bread sampled with probing tongues.

When it was over, Daphne rolled on her side, with her back to Haden, and started to weep. The bridge of flesh that connected them was flexible enough to allow a modicum of free movement.

"Are we sure this is what we want?"

Haden pressed his body against her back, clutching her stomach from behind.

"It's what we need. We're not happy. Haven't been for a while."

"I hate this."

"Here," Haden said, offering his hand. "Let's wash the

day off."

They edged to the side of the bed, sat there for a moment. Daphne wiped away the tears that traced runnels of mascara down her cheeks before standing up.

Inside the bathroom, the septic smell was almost overpowering.

"I think it's coming from under the sink," Haden said. He bent down, feeling a tug as Daphne refused to follow, pulled her down by the arm, and swung the cabinet doors open. The stench nearly knocked them over.

Squatting under the rusted belly of the sink was an animal with oily black skin. It looked like road kill with the shape of a bullfrog, which tapered whitely into something resembling a larva. The face that grinned up at Daphne and Haden was filled with teeth like heroin needles bent out of shape.

"What the fuck is that?" Haden said.

"The catalyst."

"What?" Haden burst out. "Did the Curator say something else to you?"

The animal made a noise halfway between a squeak and a croak and vomited a stream of yellow bile on the couple. As soon as it touched their skin it started to hiss and bubble.

Haden shrieked, clawed at the bile sizzling beside his left eye. Daphne made a low keening sound and wiped away the clumps on her breasts and throat. The force of their struggles sent the couple sprawling to the floor.

The animal retched, ejecting another surge of vomit, splashing the place where their bodies connected.

This was it. The separation had begun.

"Oh fuck, what do we do?" Daphne said. The words came out in a single, panting breath.

"Let it burn through."

The pain was excruciating. The slightest draft felt like a whip against the corroding flesh. The acid bore through muscle and vein, reddening the yellow froth around the wound. It trickled sluggishly and dripped on the floor with a faint plopping hiss.

The acid had melted through half the bridge of flesh, when it reached the hook joining Haden to Daphne. As soon as the first drop touched the hook, something woke up inside Haden, and his body went into revolt.

He screamed as a second hook burst through his shoulder and lunged at Daphne on a feeler of tendinous flesh.

She jerked away. The hook carved a deep gash along the ridge of her clavicle, retreated, and lunged again.

Haden grasped it in mid lash, started to pull. He could feel it tugging uncomfortably in his chest. Then there was a pop, followed by a gush of blood and lymph. The tendon came sliding out like a dead snake. Haden whipped it across the room.

The hook imbedded in Daphne's hip started to wriggle as the acid ate it away, sending a wisp of smoke into the air.

A third hook burst out of Haden's thigh, leaving a wide gash. He saw the fourth slither under the skin of his abdomen before it shot out in a vivid spray of blood. The hook wriggled free, spraying the floor and walls with red, and attacked Daphne. It raked her pubis, opening a gushing slit all the way up to her navel before penetrating the skin.

Haden went to pull it out of her, and then remembered the box cutter.

"Quick, this way!" he screamed, as the hook from his thigh lunged at Daphne, struggling for purchase.

Together they crawled naked across the floor, clawing their way into the main area. Once they reached the altar, the hook from Haden's thigh pierced the fatty tissue under Daphne's ass. She yelped in pain.

Covered in blood, looking like an overgrown miscarriage, Haden reached up and snatched the box cutter off the altar. He extended the blade and started cutting the tentacles.

When he was finished he moved to the leftover flesh connecting his body to Daphne's.

"No!" she screamed, but he ignored her and started cutting anyway.

Daphne bit her lip against the pain. Tears poured down her face. Without even knowing it, she grasped Haden's free hand and squeezed until the skin went white. With a final back and forth sawing motion, they came apart.

Haden moaned loudly and let his upper body slump to the floor. He started to cry, loud choking sobs that threatened to rip his lungs and larynx.

Daphne lay shivering on her back. Her body conveyed a network of tiny red rivers. She had never felt so cold, or so alone.

Slowly, her hand slid out of his.

The Curator entered his private museum, a vast chamber piled high with the artifacts of a million broken relationships. Peering through the eyeholes of his mask, breathing harshly, he moved toward the recent additions to his collection. Among them were two stuffed bears, one male, and the other female. He arranged them in a lewd position and started to masturbate. As he stroked himself, he remembered Haden and Daphne. How young they were. How desperate to be apart.

As he came, spraying the bears with his semen, he reflected how for Haden and Daphne, the scars of that evening in the motel would never heal. The place was redolent with loss, sadness, and pain.

The Curator couldn't imagine a better place if he tried.

Walter's Last Canvas

Paul Shrimpton

Walter Heimbach sat alone in his decidedly cramped flat.

A single, bare light bulb illuminated him overhead as he delicately added another brush stroke to the large canvas stretched out before him.

Walter was old, his face etched with a lifetime of wonders and woes. His skin was dry as parchment, marred by a prominent map of creases, laughter lines and crow's feet.

The lines ran deep. His humble surroundings told the most part of his story. He was a man with meagre belongings. Wealth had been elusive for Walter. He had always had enough to scrape by but never enough to be comfortable. A tatty, brown leather suitcase sat collecting dust on top of a scratched and bashed wardrobe. A small portable TV set nestled amongst an impressive array of tablets and medicine bottles on the bedside table. The picture rolled and flickered as canned laughter filtered out of it's tinny speakers. Dirty, thin sheets with frayed ends, haphazardly made up the single bed. No pictures of sentiment adorned the walls. His family had left the mortal world many years since. Walter led a solitary life.

No wife. No children.

A long time ago, he had a sister. But she had gone decidedly insane towards the end of her equally uneventful life. She'd been dead for ten years now. Discovered on the sofa in her front room. Hands still clutched at her throat as she choked to death before her favourite soap opera on the telly. She had succumbed to a stubborn boiled sweet lodged in her throat. Countless cats kept her corpse company for nearly a fortnight before she was found. Or what was left of her. She had been taking in feline strays for most of her adult life. And by the time of her accordingly sublime death, had an impressively sized pack of the creatures. The smell of cat shit was an overpowering and persistent odour pervading the entire house. Repulsing visitors by the time they reached the doorstep.

Few had stepped into her squalor prior her death.

The cats had resisted gnawing on their owner for five days before, half starved, they began devouring the body. Walter was duly informed of her passing.

Contact between the pair hadn't exactly been consistent over the years. The siblings had walked polar opposite paths in life. Hers one of staid, simplicity and routine whilst his was one of chaos and anarchy. Walter's many misadventures, owing largely to a heavy intake of drugs and alcohol, had led to a breakdown of his relationship to both mother and father. He'd been struck off the will and all communication severed due to one final, fateful, straw during the festive season of nineteen sixty five. A heavily intoxicated Walter announcing that he was choosing to relieve himself at the dinner table. His reaction to a less than positive debate, instigated by his sister, regarding his questionable lifestyle.

Not by accident, a lot of the steaming, dark yellow piss went over his sister. Hysterics ensued and the first and last time his father had hit Walter soon followed. He had been smacked as a child, like most children of the era, but his Father's fist connecting with Walter's adolescent nose and the spectacularly bloody aftermath drew a line between the pair that would never again be crossed.

Walter's subsequent Christmases were generally a cocktail of misguided anger, lonely self pity and loathing. All washed down of course with a bottle of whatever was strong and cheap at the time.

Walter had multiple excuses for his actions and downward spiral in life.

He was an artist. Artists were predominantly by nature unreasonable, provocative and unconventional. And, generally by definition, utter piss heads. The public actions of an imbued artist all but forgivable when fuelling a private creation of potentially groundbreaking historical merit and beauty.

Walter hadn't failed to see the irony in the outcome of his parents decision to bequeath their earthly possessions to his sister. He wasn't in the least surprised.

She would mature equally bereft of children and, quite soon after their parents passing, become notoriously known as the cat lady of Islington. The family home was ultimately inherited by the very pack of near feral cats that had consumed the softer, fleshier parts of their deceased benefactor. The added kick in the balls was that she drew more fame in her passing than Walter had collectively through his years as a struggling artist.

Walter snorted bitterly to himself, reeling in his wandering mind and turning it back to the painting. The masterpiece. He dipped the fine brush into the coloured mess on the palette gripped in his free hand. Round and thin rimmed spectacles perched too far down the length of his nose. Walter squinted into them as he applied another minuscule detail to his portrait. Glancing to the right of the canvas, intensely studying the reflection in the tall mirror. The self-portrait, whilst a work of genuine talent with pinpoint attention to detail, had a strangely unsettling quality. An underlying red hue gave the image a hellish tone. But, Walter surmised, this was an unavoidable part and parcel by-product of its creation and intention. The blank canvas, once mounted to it's sturdy wooden frame, had been graced with a generous coat of blood.

Walter's blood.

The reasoning, an alchemical process, had been outlaid in a rare book of 'Alchemy and Witchcraft' known simply as 'Diabolist', that had somehow entered Walter's possession.

He discovered it rather clumsily during a drunken frenzy, the result of throwing an empty litre bottle of cheap vodka at the wall of his very bedsit. The glass bottle didn't break but merely punched a hole through the thin plaster. The neck protruding horizontally out of it's new, snug hole in the wall. Walter had stared at it. Then shouted at it. Then finally ripped it free and successfully smashed it against the interior brickwork of the more effective, opposing, outer wall. But then, even in his heavily intoxicated and agitated state, he noticed the smell. Seeping into the room, filling it with it's cloying, repugnant odour. Walter had thrown up. Violently retching and heaving till his chest burned and his gut throbbed. Initially Walter had assumed its origin could only be the stinking flesh of a decomposing animal. Entombed between the plaster boards. A bird. Or, from a more considered observation of his surroundings, a dead rat. Walter, to his dismay, found the stench to have fantastically sobering properties, and set about the undesirable task of sticking his hand into the dark hole and searching for the damned putrescent thing. And find something he did. Walter had to break more of the plaster away to sufficiently extract the source of the stench in all its glory. His fingers brushed a soft outer skin. Hopeful fantasies of discovering hidden treasure, a trinket box perhaps, were quelled upon it's exhuming. Walter thought it was leather that the old tome was wrapped in. Until he saw the eyelid. And what looked like a lip. Stretched out of shape and bordered by an extensive array of finger prints. On the back of the book two ears provided fasteners for the human skin covering. Dried and treated the way you would another piece of quality hide.

Walter threw the macabre wrapper in the bin without hesitation. It was the book that he would keep.

Walter had heard tales of the maddened scrawls of Benvenuto Cellini. Revered Italian medieval sculptor who, after a chance encounter with a necromancer, developed a short lived interest in the black arts. The culmination of Cellini's passing passion being a scant publication of the slim 'how to' encyclopaedia of practiced and theoretical dabbling in the black arts. Near legendary in it's scarcity, owing to the book being blasted by the church as satanic and a witch hunt for copies of the book that resulted in some nice bonfires. The only presently existing 'known' copy reputedly residing in some secret location at the behest of the Vatican.

And now Walter had a copy too.

After a time consuming period of translation (he had no prior schooling of what he established to be Latin), Walter was already plotting how best to put the near mythical 'reference piece' to good use. He could make a few quid selling it on to an antiquarian dealer. Maybe more if put to auction. But the more he translated and understood, the more his curiosity transcended obsession. What if this spell book worked? This was after all the holy grail of incantations and invocations.

Having completed the prerequisites as laid out in 'Diabolist' (These consisted of utterances aloud in a language Walter couldn't pinpoint. Hoping he had pronounced the strange words correctly by mouthing aloud phonetically). Walter had then set about his masterpiece. The theory presented in the mythical tome was that upon completion of all the relevant instructions, the creator of the likeness could attain that image, that face, that physique eternally. Walter could have chosen an entirely new face and character. But fearing that would prove too weird had decided to use his own, familiar face. Not possessing any pictures of himself as a youth, Walter had opted to work from his reflection and from distant memory to paint himself as a strong, handsome twenty something. This, for Walter, proved harder than it sounded and he toiled laboriously for a good few months on the rendering. Walter set down his brush and admired his work.

Meticulous to the finest detail, Walter had just about completed what was clearly his finest work.

He lit a cigarette and let his eyes drift away from the painting. The women. That was at the forefront of his mind. He was once a lady killer, but unfortunately, age hadn't been kind to him.

He hadn't mustered an erection for at least a year now. This was the final insult to his deteriorating body and soul. There was nobody left but Marjorie. She was his home help/cleaner and current object of desire. Dowdy, heavily set and fifty. Something he wouldn't have looked twice at not too many moons ago and she presently proved to be proof in the pudding that he had indeed lost his knack. His advances were knocked back without the batting of an eyelash. Walter, a stubborn bastard, was persistent though. Maybe, when it was over, he would fuck her first, he thought. A broad, wry grin revealed the black voids of missing teeth, framed by his few remaining discoloured ones as he fantasised, picturing himself thrusting her to a noisy climax. Her skirt hitched over ripped brown nylons, robust body roughly bent double over his table as he pounded away. His grin receded as the comical image of his own bony arse and frail, liver spotted body seeped into the fantasy.

Walter stubbed out his cigarette in the overflowing pub ashtray, a handy memento stolen the last time he could afford to drink out. He coughed, a dry rattling cough that sounded potentially terminal. A glob of brown jelly coated the inside of his mouth and he toyed it's elastic texture with his tongue for a while before fumbling for something in his trouser pocket. Walter spat the offending mucus into a stained and rigid handkerchief before stuffing the filthy scrap of fabric back in his pocket for further use.

Rubbing his hands together, Walter narrowed his eyes and pursed his lips.

It was, after all, time for the final act in the ceremony.

A drastic action from Walter was required for the completion of the spell. Or should it be pact? An offering to be made to an omnipotent being of indescribable power. And to Walter's knowledge, this 'being' was of previously unknown title without the vaguest of origin. The final binding element was, predictably enough, the ultimate sacrifice. Walter didn't feel comfortable with the idea of suicide, but, if his booze ravaged mind believed in the powers held within the page of 'Diabolist' then why should he care about giving up his physical body to be reborn. A fresh start in new flesh. Walter didn't give two shits about his present, depressing state of affairs. He was passed caring years ago. Still, the unknown was a scary place to Walter. Poets had romanticised death as the greatest journey one could take. But Walter didn't want a one way fare.

What if he didn't come back?

As much as he despised everything he had become, Walter didn't want to forget what he could have been. Should have been. Heavy was such, the burden of his bitter disappointment of still having everything to prove in his mess of a so called life.

It was unquestionably a gamble.

And ultimately, when all was considered, even with so little to lose, Walter was scared.

So very, very scared.

Walter looked up at the beam running through the middle of the room, a half foot clear of the slanted ceiling.

A solid piece of timber that looked four times Walter's age and sturdy enough to support a dozen of his diminished size and frame. A thin, vertical, rope sized furrow in the wood suggested the possibility it already had. Walter took the painting carefully down from it's easel and lay it face up on the carpet before him.

Walter removed the precariously placed spectacles from the tip of his nose and placed them on his bedside table.

What the fuck was he doing? Walter shook his head and screwed his eyes tightly shut. His fist clenching into a bony, mottled ball, beating his hip softly.

He had to believe, though.

He had probably inflicted enough damage upon his body to kill himself many times over the years. That thought comforted him slightly.

Once more shouldn't hurt.

Walter stood up too quickly, grimacing at the cracking sound from his lower back. Vigorously rubbing his painting arm free of pins and needles. A dizzying fatigued sensation swept over him - causing him to sway, feet glued to the spot. Teetering back and forth like some amateur dramatic acting out a gale blown tree. His balance was threatening to depart at any given moment. Walter swallowed. Breathing in through his nose. Holding for a moment. Before exhaling a raspy rattle through his pinched slit of a mouth.

Better.

He repeated his breathing exercise until the fainting fit was safely at bay. Walter nodded to himself, satisfied he was able to kill himself safely. The irony, a mockery of self value. But Walter's values were steadfast and his determination steely. Tonight was the night he would swing from the rafters.

Walter pulled on a tatty drawer handle. The wooden furnishing spattered with years of spilt paint. Shabby without the chic. A result of being present to decades of

Walter's tormented venting upon canvas.

The length of rope that took pride of place in the open drawer had been knotted into a hangman's noose two months prior. Walter had found it coming back from the cheapest pub within staggering distance. One tatty end hanging out of a skip in the pub's car park, daring Walter to tug it. Walter had already begun the painting and at that point was still debating the best way to complete the ritual. The best course of suicide he could entertain. He had considered slashing his wrists but the idea of a less messy departure appealed to him more. Hanging seemed so much more dignified than bleeding out onto the carpet. He just had to make sure he went to the toilet beforehand. He didn't want Marjorie to see him all piss stained and shit dripping. She witnessed that from him too many times already.

The furrow around the circumference of the beam providing his makeshift gallows was already acquainted with the noose Walter held. This was where Walter had hung it from the centre of the timber to test its integrity. At least he tried to tell himself that. Deep down he knew that it was his morbid fascination that had led him to mount it just to 'see how it looked' in the room.

As the particular day he first tethered the rope to the beam progressed, he drank himself incapable of removing the noose. It hung there for a good three weeks before Walter grew sick of its company. It was distracting him from his painting.

Walter darted his gaze across the room to his bedside table.

The book. He still had to put it back in the wall.

Walter had decided in case anything went, well, wrong, then he had to safeguard his little secret. And if it went right, he still needed it safe. Walter took it over to the shoulder high hole in the far wall and unceremoniously stuffed priceless copy of 'Diabolist' into the void and pinned a painting over it.

Satisfied with his expertise in concealment, Walter dragged his small wooden chair under the furrow in the beam and peered up at it, noose dangling loosely upon the threadbare carpet from his white knuckle grip.

Here we go.

Grunting, Walter lifted one leg onto the seat of the chair. Then, resting his weight on the back of the chair, awkwardly hoisted his other leg up. Walter was somewhat alarmed to hear the chair creak it's protestations even louder than his not so finely aged bones. Walter tentatively shifted his weight from side to side and listened. The chair felt safe enough to the old man.

Old man. For now at least.

Walter's heart was beating maddeningly in his ears. At once he felt excited by the promises made within the pages of 'Diabolist', yet, equally terrified with the knowledge that he was going through with suicide. Some people hang themselves for kicks. But Walter had failed to see the attraction heralded from sexualised asphyxiation. Especially when his penis was, these days, perpetually limp. Still, if he so chose to, he could try that 'pleasure' out soon enough. If the book worked.

Walter's hands shook as he secured the rope. His mouth had gone dry and his skin prickly. Walter tugged on the noose till it had no give left. It was tied fast. He closed his eyes and slipped the loop over his head. Beads of sweat had formed upon his creased brow. One droplet trickled down over a tightly squeezed eyelid, collecting at the end of a lash like a tear. Walter gulped and sucked in a lungfull of air before sliding the slipknot down till it tickled the nape of his neck. Not too tight just yet. Walter opened his eyes, the light stinging them momentarily. He was ready. He began to count down from five in his head. He only just made it to three before one of the chair legs gave way. The chair seat tilted down to the left suddenly. Walter instinctively tried to correct his balance by leaning away from the snapping leg and grasping hold of the rope at the back of his head. He maintained a precarious foothold on the chair for a further second or two. Long enough for Walter to fleetingly doubt his actions. But it was too late. The chair toppled onto it's side with a dull, resounding thud beside his masterpiece. Walter struggled. His feet treading air below him as he swung, a human pendulum that would mercifully, shortly wind down. One of Walter's big toes connected with the side of his wardrobe, shearing a toenail in two down to the wick. It should have been agony but he didn't feel it. His neck and throat on the other hand were a different matter entirely. Although his neck was still technically unbroken, the strain of supporting his albeit slight frame had torn something within. The pain coursed his body with bursts of growing intensity. And the rope burned. Walter wanted it off. He had planned on leaping from the chair and hopefully snapping his neck. A clean break in all senses. But now he clawed desperately at the noose digging tight into his neck. His eyes bug eyed in their darkly ringed, sleep deprived sockets. Tongue engorged, lolled from his mouth and flopped over his froth splattered chin. He convulsed as he fought to take a breath. But it was futile, the rope was too tight and still squeezing tighter. His windpipe was already crushed beyond repair. Against his instincts, Walter tried to relax, to embrace the passing. He raised his arms out to each side, suspended like some absurd floating crucifixion. His head felt like it would explode. As if his skull might burst from the building pressure at any moment. His heart was pounding hard and loud, but the once steady rhythm was beginning to break down to a stuttering of oxygen starved spasmic convulsions. Veins bulged like bloody worms snaking under the surface of Walter's well worn skin. There was very little white left of his eyes, burst vessels giving his swollen oculars a horrific and hellish appearance. He could barely see anything now. The portrait below was pulling far away from him, growing dimmer, distant. Walter's weary heart was struggling, desperately fighting to muster another beat. The pain shook his very core, every limb stiffened and arched, the dribble of piss that Walter had anticipated, had leaked out and sped down his leg... and then. Floating... no, wait, was he? Was he falling? He felt weightless. Was he dead? He wasn't sure. Was this hell? He could think. And. He could reason. But had no perceptible sense, no touch, no smell. No sight. No sense that is, except that maybe he was falling.

And then he felt something cling to him. It was pleasant, reassuring. But pressing harder against his front. His face. He could feel his cheek squashed up against a surface. Fabric. He took a breath, his body quivering.

He could breathe. Walter took another and stretched out his hand, fingernails scraped on the texture beneath. A familiar texture. Tightly woven fabric he had for many moons become accustomed to waking up on. Sounds. Bird song fading into a blend of other sounds filtering through his single pane window.

Walter opened his eyes. Shapeless blobs of light dazzled his eyes with searing intensity. It was morning. The shades of white gaining colour and shape as Walter's eyes focussed. He lifted his head weakly off the carpet and took in the familiar sights of his dingy living room. His hand brushed against something hard. The portrait lay next to him. Walter instantly remembered everything and raised a hand to his throat, his fingers snagging on the noose around his neck. Walter sighed with dismay. His initial take on the circumstances being that the rope had snapped. He had passed out and the rope, for some reason or another, had simply given way. He was still Walter Heimbach, pushing eighty. He was still just a silly old man.

Walter sat up and rubbed his eyes in an effort to halt the onset of tears. He removed the noose and his suspicions confirmed by a frayed end of the snapped rope. A loose tail of rope hung from the beam still. Walter surmised it had probably rubbed on the bottom corner of the square cut wood when he was swinging. Walter pulled himself up to his feet. Straightening, stretching, he frowned. There was something missing from his actions. His back hadn't clicked. Maybe he'd jarred it into place, gravity providing the perfect remedy. Walter raised a balled hand to splutter into. A practised habit evolved from decades of smoking. He coughed. But it sounded clear. No raspy rattles. No brown solidified mucus landing upon his hand. Just a healthy, clean, cough. Walter ran a hand through his hair. All of his hair. A full, thick head of hair like he had many years ago. He noticed that his eyesight too was twenty/twenty and unaided. His glasses lay on his bedside table where he'd left them. He sniffed at the air and wrinkled his nose. The air was stagnant. And for the first time in years he could smell how truly rank his body odour was. Although revolted by the stench, Walter smiled and picked up the broken chair, setting it upright on it's remaining three legs. Walter was did his best to fetter his optimism. Temper his excitement which was swelling as he hurried into the bathroom for a good look at his reflection.

And there he was. Walter froze, his grin transformed to slack jawed wonderment. He raised a hand to his face. His smooth, soft face. Five o'clock shadow coloured his chin with patchy, adolescent inconsistency. His eyes were piercing. The whites clear and the pupils sharp. Walter bared his teeth. White, smooth, nicely formed teeth. He pulled at his shirt. Virtually ripping it from his body without haste. His skin was no longer the tired, mottled, baggy fit. It now clung tight to sinew, muscle and flesh. Abdominal muscles popped out, defined under his otherwise flat stomach. He'd never had a six pack.

Walter had that grin again.

He quickly kicked off his trousers, leaned into a small Perspex-panelled cubicle and twisted the tap to fuel the shower head. Walter didn't flinch as the cold water splashed his face. Snatching the half used soap bar from the sink he began to scrub. Erasing all trace of the old

Walter. A fresh, clean start.

Downstairs, Marjorie unlocked the front door. The streaks of morning light burst over the grim looking hallway. A set of stairs led up to the four small bedsits. She hated Fridays. And this was one of the reasons. Walter was a strange fish. A dirty old man. She had to put up with a lot of ogling from senile old men in her profession but under Walter's leering gaze she had always felt vulnerable and unnerved. That was only the half of it though. The real fear was what to expect when she opened the door. Mercifully this time of day, before ten in the morning, he was usually in a fitfully drunken sleep. Not always though. She had found him disorientated and naked on more than one occasion. Sometimes he was in an unashamed state of semi-flaccid excitement, demanding her with slurred speech to look at him. But, thankfully for small mercies that hadn't happened in a while now. She had managed to get the cleaning time of Walter's small flat down to anything between eighty minutes and three hours depending on what sort of a week Walter had endured.

She didn't feel sorry for the old piss head. He had no one. But that had been of his own doing. Driving everyone close to him far, far away with his drunken rants and humiliating outbursts. And now he was a lonely old drunk. No one would be at his funeral. Least of all Marjorie. Hell no. Marjorie gathered together her cleaning utensils from the walk in communal cupboard beneath the stairs. Dusting rags, bucket and mop at hand, Marjorie ascended the stairway. Walter's was on the top floor. God knows how the old fart hadn't killed himself staggering up and down those stairs. Maybe it was that exercise that was keeping him going. Climbing to the top floor. God knows it was already taking it's toll on Marjorie's knees. She huffed and puffed for breath as she struggled with mop and bucket, a silent display of exaggerated toil to an invisible audience. Look how hard I have it. Look at me, struggling up these bastard stairs for some decrepit old piece of shit. And for what? Minimum wage? Fuck that.

Marjorie stopped outside a grubby white door. The paint chipped. A brown stain from filthy hands searching for the lock spread out in a wide fading circle from the Yale keyhole. The doormat had what looked like old pasta and an indiscernible variety of mouldy fruit squashed and ingrained into its bristled ridges. This was unmistakably Walter's front door. Marjorie had her own key. She didn't knock. Hopefully, if he was asleep, he wouldn't wake. She tentatively tiptoed into the small parlour room and stooped to place the bucket and mop on the floor. She could already hear the shower running. This presented all manner of potential scenarios developing in Marjorie's head. All that is, with an underlying basis of enabling Walter opportunistically exposing himself to his cleaner in some shape or form.

Fucking pervert.

Marjorie took a deep breath and quietly proceeded into the kitchen and began to run the hot water tap into the bucket. Maybe it'll affect the water flow in the bathroom, cause the old bastard to scald his pathetic bits or chill them down to an innocuous size. Marjorie refused to regard Walter's manhood as a cock or anything akin to sexualising that limp thing he sometimes waggled at her with glazed eyes and spit flecked mouth. Only a wine stained vest offered her eyes (if she were lucky) protection from his revolting body. She should have reported him but he always paid a little tip for the disservice. She needed the money. Marjorie tightened the tap, stemming the water. It was visibly hot, spewing steam through a delicate foam of soapy suds. Marjorie lifted the bucket out of the sink with a guttural grunt as she tried not to slop water. Marjorie padded quietly through to the living room.

She saw it immediately. Looking up at her from the centre of the room. Beautiful. The perfect rendering of a perfect specimen. Marjorie had momentarily lost herself in the picture on the floor. Sucked into those deep blue eyes, penetrating her core. The striking jawline, the finely shaped cheekbones, the body. Toned and sun kissed. Marjorie shifted her body to rest the bucket of water on the chair next to her. The broken chair, unstable on it's three legs toppled immediately. The bucket hurtled down onto the bewitching painting, water splashed wide across the masterpiece and formed a puddle in the water resistant surface. The color drained from Marjorie's face. Shit. Marjorie looked around the room desperately searching for a means to soak up the incriminating puddle. There was a towel poking out of the dresser drawer. Without hesitating she whipped it out and advanced toward the portrait.

Walter marvelled at his body as he showered. He was burning with excitement. With the book he would further his destiny. It had worked. It. Had. Worked! He could make money, so much money. From the right people. Combining his artistry with the magic of the book. He could make a whole lot of money. A lot of old rich folk out there. Too old to fully enjoy their spoils without his help. Walter grinned and threw back his head, letting the water splash his face.

Marjorie stood poised over the painting, a towel clutched and outstretched, threatening the puddle of water. Marjorie doubted she knew how she could clean it best. Hopefully she could lay the towel flat and absorb the water, then peel it off. But what if the paint peeled away with the towel? Maybe she should rub it. Maybe. If the paint was dry, maybe it had a crusty shell, like the cheap acrylics she used in her art classes at school did when they dried out. She had saved one of those before from a water splash. Kind of. She had to do something. Marjorie stooped low and pressed down with the towel over the handsome but submerged face in the painting.

Without warning and quite an amount of force, Walter's perfect new face burst open like a surrealists interpretation of popping a blister. The action was with shocking abruptness and explosive results as a rich tapestry of brightly coloured fluid coated the inside of the shower panels. His nose, eyes, cheeks, mouth, disintegrated in a millisecond. Walter felt no pain as such. Confused, he froze for a second. His hands raised, pressed against the tiled back walls of the small bathroom. His face, or what was left of his face, gushed multicoloured fluids wildly into the cubicle. The vivid hued 'blood' spewed in torrents from the moist, fleshy chasm where Walter's face had departed. It's epicentre where the nose had been, but the void was far reaching, from ear to ear and chin to brow. The outline of a head remained but it was housing a pit of raw meat pissing colours. All the colours of the rainbow.

It's gone dark.

That was all that ran through Walter's mind at first. Maybe he'd blacked out and was dreaming. He couldn't smell anything. He had nothing to smell with. He tried to open his mouth. To shout. But nope, no mouth either. He could feel though. The water still pattered down on him. He could feel it's warmth. Even warmer waters still, were trickling over his chest. Walter blindly raised a hand to his faceless maw and slowly reached out a finger to feel. The extended digit twitched in the air expectantly but there was nothing to make contact with. Walter kept pushing his hand further, seeking face, until finally he felt something beneath his fingers. A cloying, moist putty, deep within his skull. His fingers ploughed through the colourful, jelly like flesh. The water from the shower head swilled more of the quickly dissolving bone, meat and sinew out of the shelf like base of a chin. Walter moved his hand out before him. It was full of the vibrant flesh, slowly he raised it level with his former eye line as if to examine its contents. He couldn't see the wild splashes of vivacious hues cascading from out of his upturned palm but the damage to Walter's loose grip on his faculties had been done. Walter's mind had finally snapped entirely.

Marjorie stared down at the portrait, horrified. Where the beautifully executed, handsomely alluring face of the subject had been there was now a random, smudged, mix of colour. Reds, greens, blues, whites and blacks swirled and blended to make something that looked like Van Gogh's puke after a heavy night on the absinthe and advocaat. Marjorie tried to fix it, clearly not thinking through her actions, she again pressed down with the towel and rubbed.

Walter was still stood motionless in the shower, his mind reeling from losing his face, confused and disorientated by the abrupt lack of vital senses. When, without warning, his right arm and shoulder exploded in a spectacular gout of colour, instantaneously liquified and bursting in all directions. The white tiles were momentarily awash with fresh glorious splashes before it was showered away, down into the drain. Glugging through flaked skin and matted cotters of hair from a Walter of old. Not that Walter noticed. He was past fear, beyond rational thought in a vacuous limbo of insanity. Then his whole torso, head and remaining arm were gone. They popped simultaneously. Yet more colour briefly adorned the walls. Walter's legs crumpled on the plastic shower tray shortly afterward. Lifeless, still joined tenuously at the crotch. They soon were gone too. Disintegrating, exploding, dissolving, diluting.

Marjorie stood over the painting. She had rubbed and wiped it down to the bare canvas in parts. Elsewhere the paint had simply been smudged into a formless oblivion. Only the background in far corners remained untouched. The familiar dirty walls of Walter's room. If Marjorie had been of an inquisitive nature and had a keen eye for details she may have noticed the hole in the wall painted in shadowy detail on the ruined portrait. She may have observed this and deduced that it was the location of a clue to the puzzle. But Marjorie didn't harness any of these problem solving attributes. Sleuth she was not. And she didn't care enough about Walter to give it much presence of thought. If anything she was fearful of how he would react to her meddling of his work. She left in a hurry and never returned. The destroyed painting was binned, finally crushed and ripped to shreds, it's tattered remains buried in a landfill five miles east of the city. Sometimes Marjorie did think about the painting. The wondrously handsome man. Sometimes she would dream about him.

Walter, unnoticed in his absence was soon forgotten about. Only his landlord became aware of his tenant's departure when the sporadic installments of rent payments ceased altogether. The landlord was grateful. Glad to have finally gotten rid of the drunk who annoyed his neighbours with his boarish ways. Whether dead or alive no one knew and no one cared. No tombstone to merit the merest hint of a legacy, Walter's work was destroyed before it left his flat in life by his own hands and in death at the hands of strangers. The few possessions of Walter's found temporary shelter in a skip before disposal, or if holding slight value, the back pocket of the unlucky sod given the job of clearing out the stinking hovel.

The book was never recovered. The hole in the wall never investigated. Patched up by a decorator priming the flat for the next tenant. The book could wait, it would be held again. And it's powers within, would never grow old.

Contributors

Jeff Burk is the cult favorite author of Shatnerquake, Super Giant Monster Time, Cripple Wolf, and Shatnerquest. Like the literary equivalent to a cult B-Horror movie, Burk writes violent, absurd, and funny stories about punks, monsters, gore, and trash culture. Everyone normally dies at the end. He is also the Head Editor of *Eraserhead Press'* horror imprint, *Deadite Press*. Born in the Pennsylvania backwoods, he was raised on a steady diet of Godzilla, Star Trek, and EC Comics. He now resides in Portland, Oregon. His influences include: Sleep deprivation, comic books, drugs, magick, and kittens.

Nathan Robinson lives in Scunthorpe with his darling five year old twin boys and his patient wife/editor. So far he's had numerous short stories published by *www.spinetinglers.co.uk*, *Rainstorm Press*, *Knight Watch Press*, *Pseudopod*, *The Horror Zine*, *The Sinister Horror Company*, *Static Movement*, *Splatterpunk Zine* and many more. He writes best in the dead of night or travelling at 77mph. He is a regular reviewer for *www.snakebitehorror.co.uk*, which he loves because he gets free books. He likes free books. His first novel Starers was released by *Severed Press* to rave reviews. This was followed by his short story collection Devil Let

Me Go, and the novellas Ketchup With Everything and Midway. He is currently working on his next novels, Caldera, Death-Con 4 and a sequel to Starers. Follow news, reviews and the author blues at *www.facebook.com/NathanRobinsonWrites* or twitter *@natthewriter*

Robert Essig is the author of In Black, People of the Ethereal Realm, and Through the In Between, Hell Awaits. He has also published over seventy short stories, two novellas, and edited two anthologies. Robert lives with his family in Southern California.

Jeff Strand is a four-time nominee (and zero-time winner) of the Bram Stoker Award. His novels include Pressure, Dweller, Wolf Hunt, and a bunch of others. You can visit his *Gleefully Macabre* website at *www.jeffstrand.com*

Saul Bailey lives in Barnstaple, North Devon, surrounded by alcoholics and pubs. If that sounds like fun, he's telling it wrong. Moving is too expensive and suicide too much effort. That leaves writing. So he writes.

Adam Cesare's books include Zero Lives Remaining, The First One You Expect, Video Night, The Summer Job, Mercy House and Tribesmen. He writes a monthly column exploring horror fiction and film for *Cemetery Dance Online*. He lives in Philadelphia and can be found at AdamCesare.com, where he's giving away a free ebook if you sign up for his mailing list.

Shane McKenzie is the author of many horror and bizarro books, including Muerte Con Carne, Pus Junkies, and Wet And Screaming. He wrote comics for *Zenescope Entertainment*. His novel Muerte Con Carne was adapted into a multiple award winning short film called EL Gigante, which will be a feature film very soon. He lives in Austin, TX with his wife and two children.

Brendan Vidito is a short story author and novelist from Sudbury, Ontario. He studied literature in university and collaborated on the publication of a local literary journal. His work has appeared in *Splatterpunk Zine, Dark Moon Digest,* and *Infernal Ink Magazine*. He's paranoid, eats too much cheese, and sells his excessive body hair to help make Chewbacca Halloween costumes for kids. You can visit him at *brendanvidito.wordpress.com*

Paul Shrimpton is been a lifelong horror fan. He has dabbled in filmmaking - winning the Horror Channel's: *Cut! Short Horror Film* competition (in 2008 with the revenge quickie Hung Up and in 2009 with the zombie ridden Teleportal). Teleportal subsequently gained inclusion in the *Dread Central* feature anthology Zombieworld. Paul also co-wrote the 2011 comedy horror Inbred and recently performed writing duties on the (at time of writing) forthcoming splatter comedy, Attack of the Adult Babies. Paul also plays Bass guitar in the horror film tinged ska-punk outfit *Deadbeat At Dawn*. This is his first published short story.

Dan Henk was born in 1972, on a small army base in the south, he grew up on a diet of science fiction and horror books. At eighteen Dan Henk was kicked out of his house. He spent the next eight months homeless, often living in the woods. Six months later, he was in the passenger seat of a car that flipped and his face broke the windshield. Soon after that, the tendon on his thumb was severed in a fight with a crackhead. He came down with brain cancer in 2001, and his wife died in a hit-and-run in 2007. In 2012, a car shattered his bike, throwing him through the windshield and putting him in a coma for hours. There's a running theory that he is a cyborg. He's done art for *Madcap Magazine, Maximum Rock and Roll Magazine, Tattoo Artist Magazine, Black Static, This is Horror, Deadite Press, Skin Deep, The Living Corpse, Aphrodesia, Splatterpunk, Tattoo*

Prodigies, Pint Sized Paintings, Coalesce, Zombie Apocalypse, Most Precious Blood, Indecision, Locked In A Vacancy, Shai Hulud, Purity Records, and a slew of *Memento* books. 2011 saw the release of his first book, The Black Seas of Infinity, care of *Anarchy Books*. *Permuted Press* reissued it in 2015, and a few months later released his second novel Down Highways in the Dark...By Demons Driven.

Jack Bantry is the editor of *Splatterpunk Zine*. He works as a postman and resides in a small town at the edge of the North York Moors.

Printed in Great Britain
by Amazon